AND THE
CLASH WITH FATHER
TIME

BOOK DEP $ 14·83

ALSO BY MICHAEL PANCKRIDGE

MICHAEL PANCKRIDGE

with BRETT LEE

Toby Jones

—— AND THE ——
CLASH WITH FATHER TIME

Angus&Robertson
An imprint of HarperCollins*Publishers*

All references to *Wisden Cricketers' Almanack* are by kind permission of
John Wisden & Co. Ltd.

Angus&Robertson

An imprint of HarperCollins*Publishers*, Australia

First published in Australia in 2007
by HarperCollins*Publishers* Australia Pty Limited
ABN 36 009 913 517
www.harpercollins.com.au

HarperCollins*Publishers*

25 Ryde Road, Pymble, Sydney NSW 2073, Australia
31 View Road, Glenfield, Auckland 10, New Zealand
77–85 Fulham Palace Road, London W6 8JB, United Kingdom
2 Bloor Street East, 20th floor, Toronto, Ontario M4W 1A8, Canada
10 East 53rd Street, New York, NY 10022, USA

Panckridge, Michael, 1962-.
    Toby Jones and the clash with Father Time.
    For children aged 10-14 years.
    ISBN 978 02072 0047 2 (pbk).
    1. Cricket – Juvenile fiction. I. Lee, Brett. II. Title.
A 823.4

Cover photography by Alex Jennings; cricket memorabilia by Sport
Memorabilia, Sydney Antique Centre; clock image by Shutterstock Images
Illustrations on pages vi–vii by Steven Bray
Typeset in 10/15pt Stone Serif by Helen Beard, ECJ Australia Pty Limited
Printed and bound in Australia by Griffin Press
60gsm Bulky Paperback used by HarperCollins*Publishers* is a natural, recyclable
product made from wood grown in a combination of sustainable plantation and
regrowth forests. It also contains up to a 20% portion of recycled fibre. The
manufacturing processes conform to the environmental regulations in Tasmania,
the place of manufacture.

5 4 3 2 1   07 08 09 10

To Jo, Eliza and Bronte, who have supported the entire Toby Jones five-book 'cricket match', with patience, enthusiasm and love.

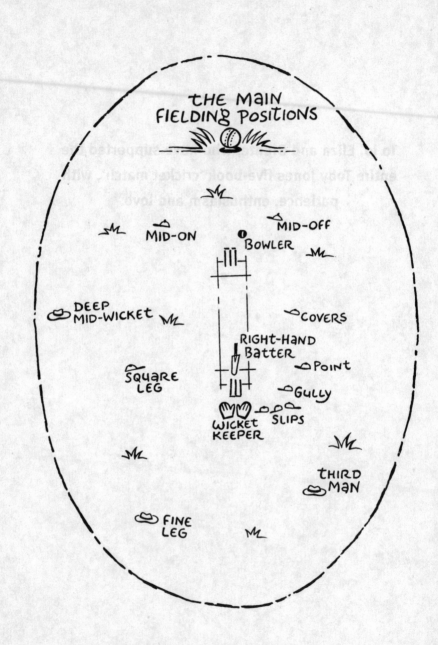

tHE MAIN
FIELDING POSITIONS

MID-ON   MID-OFF

                    BOWLER

DEEP
MID-WICKET   COVERS

                    RIGHT-HAND
                    Batter

SQUARE   POINT
LEG
                              GULLY

                              SLIPS
WICKET
KEEPER

                                    tHIRD
                                    MAN

        FINE
        LEG

CLOSE UP OF the CENTRE WICKET

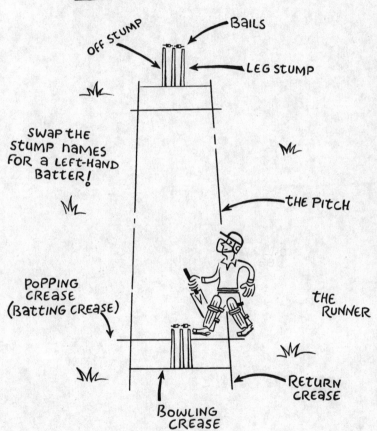

OFF STUMP

BAILS

LEG STUMP

SWAP the STUMP NAMES FOR a LEFT-HAND BATTER!

the PITCH

POPPING CREASE (BATTING CREASE)

the RUNNER

BOWLING CREASE

RETURN CREASE

Foreword

JUST like Toby Jones, I was obsessed by the game of cricket when I was a kid. I was always looking for ways to improve my game. I learned so much from my older brother Shane, and from seeking the advice of coaches. I read every cricket book I could get my hands on and I watched and learned from my idol: Dennis Lillee. Dennis was my inspiration, someone who I looked up to. I wanted to be just like him. (As it turned out, he has had a lot to do with my cricket career.)

I am sure you will find that this book is not only an excellent read, but also a very useful guide to the game of cricket. It contains lots of great hints and information that I hope you will be able to use to improve your own game.

When I first became involved in cricket, I had no idea where the game would take me. The opportunities and possibilities it has created for me are endless. Cricket has taught me many valuable lessons. Most of all it has shown me that if I always play hard and *enjoy* the opportunity of representing my country, I will be successful.

Every time I get asked to offer cricket advice to kids, my answer is always the same: enjoyment is the most important part of the game. When I am on the field, you will nearly always find me with a huge smile on my face. After suffering several injuries in my younger years, I have learned to make the most of every moment I get to play cricket.

This book reminds me of my own childhood days spent in the backyard with my brothers, always battling hard on the pitch to see who would be the champion player at the end of the day.

The *Toby Jones* series brings back truly great memories for me. I hope you enjoy reading *Toby Jones and the Clash with Father Time*.

Brett Lee

Prologue

What wonders abound, dear boy, don't fear
These shimmering pages, never clear.
Choose your year, the Wisden name,
Find the page, your destined game,
Then find yourself a quiet place
Where shadows lurk, to hide your trace.

Whisper clear date, place or score
While staring, smitten; then before
(You hope) the close of play,
Be careful now, you've found the way.
So hide your home, your age, your soul
To roam this place and seek your goal.

Be aware that time moves on —
Your time, this time; none short, or long.
So say aloud two lines from here
Just loud enough for you to hear.
From a quiet spot, alone, unknown,
Back through time, now come — alone.

And never speak and never boast,
And never taunt, nor ever toast
This knowledge from your time you bring.
To woo the rest, their praises sing:
They wonder, and your star shines bright . . .
Just this once, this one short night?

But every word that boasts ahead
Means lives unhinged, broken, dead.
Don't meddle, talk, nor interfere
With the lives of those you venture near.
Respect this gift. Stay calm, stay clever.
And let the years live on forever.

1 Grubbers

'Toby, get your eyes off the screen and back on the pitch here. Anyone would think you were in next.' Glenn Mason tossed me the ball and pointed to the net.

'Actually, I hope I don't even get a bat,' I replied, spinning the ball in my hand. 'Jimbo and Cam are looking solid.'

I was down in the indoor nets at the MCG bowling to our number four and five batters. Out on the ground the Aussie openers were making a solid start in our two-day 'Ashes' Test match against a team from England.

'What's the score?' Sean, our captain, called from the other end. I glanced at Glenn then stole another quick peek at the screen. It still gave me goose bumps to see Jimbo's and Cam's name at the bottom of the screen with the current scores alongside.

'Thirty-one,' I called. 'Jimbo just plastered a four through wide mid-on.'

'I wouldn't be surprised to see that kid back out there in ten years with the real baggy green on his head,' one of the coaches muttered to Glenn. I pretended not to hear, though I couldn't wait to tell Jimbo.

Off a half run-up I bowled down about three overs to Sean; mainly gentle half-volleys and good length deliveries that he could get on the front foot to and hit firmly and crisply into the side netting. I'm sure it was a good way to build up his confidence, as he was hitting the ball so sweetly.

'That'll do,' Sean soon called. As he was walking towards me we heard a shout and then a groan from upstairs. I raced over to the screen.

'They got Cam,' Glenn said, frowning. 'I reckon that hit his pad outside off-stump.' We watched Cam walk quickly from the ground. He had arrived from some remote country town for the cricket camp which had started last week. There were rumours that he'd never played for a real cricket team; just with his brothers and mates in the street outside his home. I'd noticed him struggling with the thigh pad and helmet; maybe he'd never worn them before.

'Never seen a batter more happy about getting out,' muttered Marty, another of our coaches.

'He's just thrilled to be here,' Glenn said, smiling despite the wicket. He leant in closer to watch the replay of Cam's dismissal. As I was a fast bowler I was

2

pretty familiar with the lbw laws. If a ball hit the pad outside off-stump, you could only be out lbw if you weren't playing a shot.

'He played a shot at that, didn't he?' Marty nodded, not taking his eyes from the screen. 'He got his bat a bit caught up in his pads. Maybe the umpire thought he was padding up.'

'Benefit of the doubt should have gone to the batter,' I said. 'And it looks like it could have been high. I reckon that was going over the stumps anyway.' Marty and Glenn turned to look at me. I noticed Glenn's slight smile.

'I heard you knew a bit about the game.' Glenn nodded in approval. 'And that's a very good thing. Now get back upstairs and learn some more by watching.' I left the two of them in front of the screen and trotted back upstairs.

'Toby, my boy,' a voice called.

'Jim!' I jogged over to the old man who had introduced me to time travel and sat down next to him. Because of Jim I had been on some amazing cricketing adventures, using the *Wisden* to go back in time to cricket matches in the past.

'My dear Toby . . .'

'Oh no!' I interrupted, as we both watched our number three batsman get clean-bowled for a golden duck. Jim turned to me and smiled.

'Cricket does have a habit of knocking you down just when you . . .' For a moment I wasn't aware that Jim had stopped talking. I was too busy watching the replay up on the big screen. Callum's off-stump had been knocked out of the ground, cartwheeling back and almost collecting the England wicketkeeper. I groaned, then turned to look at Jim.

'Jim?' He didn't reply. 'Jim, are you okay?'

'Good Lord,' he muttered, suddenly reaching down beneath his seat. He pulled out an old brown case.

'What is it, Jim? What can you see?' He raised a pair of ancient-looking binoculars to his eyes. His wrinkled hands were shaking slightly. For a moment I thought he might have spotted the England players doing a bit of ball tampering but he wasn't gazing at the players celebrating alongside the wicket. 'I thought you were heading off anyway,' I said, still trying to get his attention.

'I wonder,' he said softly. Then he shook his head. 'Impossible.'

'Jim, please! What are you talking about?' Finally Jim put the glasses down and turned to me.

'Toby, the Timeless Cricket Match. You remember?'

'How could I forget,' I said, shivering at the thought. The Timeless Cricket Match was a game being played in a strange and distant place. Not even Jim knew its whereabouts. I had ended up there with the Cricket Lord, Hugo Malchev, and if it hadn't been for Jim and a couple of my friends I might still be there. It was a cold, desolate and spooky place where strange creatures like ghosts hovered around a never-ending cricket match being played by old, weary-

4

looking players. The game had been going forever. Jim had said that if the game ever stopped, so would the real game of cricket.

'Toby, I feared as much when we came back from that despicable place. That figure on the ground?' He was pointing to a distant section of the oval. I could just make out the faint image of someone moving. I leant forward in my seat. 'They are Grubbers.'

'Grubbers? As in a ball that rolls along the pitch?'

'I'm not exactly sure who coined the phrase,' he said, looking around the ground anxiously. I followed his gaze to the other side of the oval but could see nothing but green grass and the England players taking up their positions for the hat-trick delivery.

'Let's just pause a moment,' he said, as we watched the England pace bowler charging in from the Southern end. Sean got onto the front foot and drove it majestically through the covers for a two. Despite Jim's worried frown I smiled. It was an exact replica of the shots he'd been playing off my deliveries downstairs in the nets only a few minutes ago.

'You were saying?' I was only giving Jim fifty per cent of my attention. I glanced at the scoreboard again. We were 2–38 and needing a partnership.

'The Grubbers have a two-fold purpose.'

'Who or what exactly are Grubbers?' I asked. I remembered the mysterious figures that had been floating around the edge of the ground, swarming and swooping like vultures, when I'd last been at the Timeless Cricket Match.

'They are the souls of long-dead cricketers, Toby.'

'Are they good?'

'They are neither good nor evil. They are in a state of nothingness. As I said, their purpose is to keep the Timeless Cricket Match alive by being there. They are the souls of dead cricketers. As long as there are spectators, the game of cricket survives. But they are there for another reason too.'

'And it's a Grubber out there? What does he want here? What will he do?'

'Well, like anyone who has once played this mighty game and suddenly sees the opportunity to again, he wants to play cricket.'

'So, why doesn't he?'

'Oh, he will, Toby, he will. But he will do so by taking over the physical body of a current player.' Jim lifted the glasses to his eyes again, scanning the field. 'Lost him, or else I was perhaps mistaken. Let us hope so.'

'But how?' I was finding it hard to imagine that anything sinister could happen as the sun suddenly burst from behind a cloud and the ground lit up.

'They look real enough, these Grubbers,' Jim continued, 'but they are in fact spirits determined to play cricket again; or at least be a part of the game, as spectators. It's a complicated process but possession of a body is rapid, and very hard to reverse the longer it is established. And the more time they have ownership of that person, the harder it is to detect that a possession even took place.'

'Sounds pretty weird to me.' I applauded loudly as Jimbo cover-drove a half-volley past point for an easy two.

'The personalities blend together over time, so I'm told, though I have no direct experience of it myself. You see, the Grubbers have only ever escaped the Timeless Cricket Match once before, and then we were able to contain the situation fairly quickly.'

Polite applause rippled around the ground as the England bowler took his blue cap from the umpire. We had collapsed from 0–35 to 2–41 in the space of an over. Jim turned to face me. This time I turned too and met his eyes. He looked tired suddenly.

'Toby, the Grubbers are also keeping perhaps the most evil being ever known captive in the scoreboard there.'

'That big old scoreboard at the Timeless Cricket Match? Who?'

Jim glanced at the enormous new MCG scoreboard and smiled sadly.

'That big old scoreboard you refer to, my boy, is the most beautiful structure I know. A glorious monument to cricket that has withstood the test of time like nothing else.' I glanced past Jim to the scoreboard which was now showing a replay of the last dismissal.

'But the old scoreboard can't show replays,' I said, quietly.

'Ah, Toby.' Jim shook his head sadly. He sighed and turned to me, his face solemn. 'Inside that old scoreboard is Father Time.'

'Father Time?' Jim had mentioned such a figure and of course I knew about the old weather vane at Lord's in England. 'Father Time's real?'

'Father Time is very real,' Jim said, his lips pursed. 'But he is not the benign old father figure most people think he is.' Jim glanced about as if someone might be listening close by. He lowered his voice. 'Father Time almost crushed the game many years ago but the Cricket Lords managed to capture him. A powerful spell now has him permanently trapped in the scoreboard, scoring the Timeless Cricket Match. And for every Grubber there is a keeper, ensuring that he stays in his rightful place — doomed to score cricket forever. He has immense power, but thankfully it cannot be utilised while he is controlled. But should he ever break free, he has the power to distort the time of anyone he comes into contact with.'

'What do you mean?'

'Think of an autumn leaf, fluttering as it falls from a tree; sometimes forward, sometimes backwards, before eventually coming to rest on the ground. Under Father Time's spell you are as powerless as that leaf; flitting forward in time then suddenly flicking back into the past. By the time you come to rest on the ground, your life has become a blur of unimaginable encounters and fractures. He is a very dangerous being, Toby.'

Another shout of joy erupted from the oval. I felt the butterflies jumping in my stomach as I waited for the umpire to give his decision. Slowly he raised his right index finger.

'Oh no,' I groaned. 'Jim, I better go pad up.'

'Yes, yes, my boy. Don't you worry yourself about Father Time and the Grubbers. I'm sure I was mistaken.'

We both looked around the field. There was no one out there but rejoicing England players and the umpires.

'Anyway, the umpire will just tell them to get off the field,' I said, standing up.

'Well, he would, if the umpire could in fact see the Grubber.'

'But *you* can see it?'

'And you, Toby. I perhaps more clearly than you given that I'm a Cricket Lord.'

'Do you think you were mistaken, Jim?' I asked, nervously.

'Toby, a visitor to the Timeless Cricket Match has a one-way ticket. No one is supposed to leave once they arrive. The crowd there should be slowly filling with each passing of a Test cricketer. But we left and have created a hole.'

I wasn't following him. 'A hole?'

'An escape channel.'

'You mean those Grubber people are leaving?' I stopped, suddenly forgetting the game out on the oval. Jim nodded slowly.

'And if they leave, there is no one there to watch the game,' I continued, following Jim's train of thought. 'And if there's no one there, the game stops.'

'Yes, Toby.'

'And . . .'

'Off you go, Toby. Keep your head down and each ball on its merit, do you hear?'

I nodded, barely registering Jim's words of advice.

2 Pitch Invasion

Saturday — afternoon

'Toby!' I turned to see Georgie, Ally and the others running towards me.

'Hey!' I called, distracted. I wanted to get inside and put on my pads; maybe have a hit down in the nets.

'Toby, good luck,' Georgie said. She passed me a neat-looking leather wristband. 'I made it for you last week.'

'Thanks, Georgie. I'd better go, guys. We're under the pump.'

'Toby!' Ally caught my arm and gave me a quick kiss on the cheek. 'You're the best, Tobes. Get out there and show 'em.' I felt myself suddenly go red. I turned away quickly, wondering whether Georgie had heard. She certainly wouldn't have missed the kiss. I stopped and turned, wanting to talk to Georgie. I had barely thanked her. But Marty, our coach, was shouting at me to get a move on.

11

Taking a deep breath, I entered the dressing room. Scott Craven, our brilliant all-rounder but all-round ugly guy, bumped past me, knocking me off balance.

'Watch out, Jones,' he growled.

'This guy bowling from the other end is deceptively quick,' Marty was explaining, as I grabbed my kit. Trying to steady my shaking hands, I hauled out my pads and sat down next to Marty who was staring at a small TV screen. 'His arm action is fast but he runs in slow and easy.'

Strapping on my pads I kept an eye on the screen.

'He's got a good slower ball too,' I commented. Marty nodded. I got up and moved to the back of the dressing room to put on my protector and thigh pad, missing our second duck of the innings. We were collapsing like tenpins.

'You want a hit?' Cam asked me. I don't think the huge grin had left his face since he'd arrived here on Monday morning.

'No thanks, Cam. I might just sit here and watch for a bit.'

Usually I liked to walk around to be behind the bowler's arm so I could see if there was any movement happening, but that wasn't so easy at the MCG. I can remember one of the TV cricket commentators saying that the bowling always looks faster if you're watching from side on. The England bowlers were certainly looking sharp at the moment and their team was full of noise and confidence as Scott Craven faced up.

I glanced at the clock. There was another forty minutes before lunch. Scott survived the rest of the over and I leant forward in my seat as I watched Jimbo come down and chat with him. We were 4–41 and needed to survive till lunch. Scott was an impulsive hitter; he could tear an attack apart. He was the Kevin Pietersen of our side. I wasn't sure whether it was the best advice to tell Scott to slow down. It was against his natural instincts.

The players' room was hushed and tense as we watched our fifth wicket pair slowly build the score. With twenty minutes to go before lunch England brought on their spinner. I had all but forgotten my conversation with Jim as he trotted in to bowl. Crack. It sounded like a rifle shot echoing around the stadium. Scott had clubbed him over mid-wicket for an enormous six.

'That nearly hit the fence on the full,' Marty said, trying to contain his excitement. Someone else let out a low whistle. Scott did it again with the fourth ball of the over, this time over wide mid-on. We stood up and applauded.

'Steady, big feller,' Tom Gilbert, another one of our coaches, said. I hadn't noticed him sneak into the room. He settled in next to me.

'Every ball on its merits,' he said softly. The England captain adjusted the field, pushing another man out near the fence.

'He's challenging him,' I said. 'And Scott loves a challenge.'

Tom shook his head. 'This is a real test for him. That lad's not bowling cream pies.'

My mind raced back to Adam Gilchrist during the 2006–07 Ashes series. He'd hit three sixes off Monty Panesar on his way to the second-fastest Test hundred ever. Was Scott going to be as good a hitter as Gilchrist?

The next ball was pitched shorter and a little quicker. I watched in awe as Scott charged down the pitch, aiming to smack another ball into the stands, but the ball dipped and dropped quickly, spinning past his flashing blade. The keeper took it cleanly and whipped off the bails before Scott had time to turn around, let alone get back into his crease. The square leg umpire didn't even need the third umpire.

Someone in the front row of our room swore loudly.

'I don't want to see you till lunchtime, you hear?' Marty snapped through gritted teeth. Wiping my sweaty hands on my shirt I grabbed my helmet, gloves and bat and left the room. Taking a few deep breaths to try and settle my nerves I walked down towards the ground.

'Right arm over, one ball to come,' the umpire called as I settled over my bat. I had taken guard and had a good long look around the field.

'One ball,' I murmured to myself as I waited for the bowler to step up to the crease. I watched his spinning hand carefully as he delivered the ball. I could hear it fizz as it spun through the air. It pitched outside off-stump and spun further away. I had survived.

'Nothing stupid, Toby,' Jimbo said, meeting me halfway down the pitch. 'They're good bowlers, all of them.'

Jimbo and I managed to see off the last five overs before lunch but didn't make much impact on the scoreboard. I glanced up at it on our way off. The huge screen was showing the replay of the last ball I faced; a glide through a vacant fourth slip that sped to the boundary.

'That could so easily have been caught,' I muttered to Jimbo, taking off my helmet.

'Yeah, but it wasn't, Toby. That's all that matters.'

We had lunch together with the England players and coaching staff, though only the adults mingled. Jimbo and I found a seat together and planned a humungous partnership that would take us through till tea.

'Boys?' Marty put a hand on each of our shoulders. He sat down opposite us. 'I can't tell you enough how important your partnership is to our fortunes — Australia's fortunes. This is not club cricket. This is an Australia–England Test match at the MCG.' I felt a thrill run through me as I looked at the passion on his face. 'You are there, boys. Now. Right now. Most kids would give their eye teeth to be playing for their country, let alone at the home of cricket. Enjoy it, but work your butts off getting Australia back into this game.'

Jimbo and I said nothing. We knew what we had to do. I wasn't going to go into my shell. England had done that in 2006 in Adelaide during the Ashes series and Australia had romped home on the last day to snatch an improbable victory.

'Shall I try and give you the strike, Jimbo?' Jimbo was swirling his arms around in gigantic windmill circles as we walked back out onto the ground.

'No way, Toby. We do this together.' We touched gloves. 'Hey, did you make that?'

I followed Jimbo's gaze up to the second tier of the Southern Stand. An enormous banner with 'TOBY JONES' written in green and gold letters was hanging over the edge. Noticing me looking up towards them, some kids waved frantically.

'Geez, when did they do that?' Jimbo, marching purposefully towards his end, didn't hear me.

We played carefully for the next twenty minutes and I was just beginning to really relax and enjoy myself out in the middle of the MCG when something caught my eye behind the square leg umpire; just inside the boundary. No one else seemed at all interested but I was certain I had seen someone or something — a tall man standing a few metres inside the fence. At the end of the over Jimbo and I met mid-pitch again.

'Did you notice the guy come onto the field?' I asked him, pointing out through the covers. Jimbo shrugged.

'Could have been one of the England coaches bringing out some water,' he said. He was more interested in the state of the game. 'Another five overs, Toby. Let's do it in five sets.'

'Yup, and back up for the singles. That tall guy at mid-on is pretty slow.'

'Agreed.' We touched gloves again. I glanced back towards the fence. The man had reappeared. He was standing still and resolute, his arms by his sides.

'Who's the guy down by the fence?' I asked the umpire, pointing with my bat out past square leg.

'Which guy?' The umpire looked at me quizzically.

'That guy.'

'Not sure who you mean, son,' he said, dropping his left arm to signal for the bowler that he was ready and settling into his position. I looked again. The man had taken a few paces forward. I turned back to concentrate on the play, just leaving my crease as the bowler delivered. Jimbo fended the ball off his hip down behind square leg.

'Yes!' I called, heading off down the pitch for the leg bye. I kept an eye on the man as I jogged through. He had paused again, staring transfixed at the action on the pitch.

'On its merit,' I mumbled to myself, tapping my bat in the crease and trying to put the man out of my mind. I forced a couple of twos through the off-side and punched the last delivery off my toes through mid-wicket. Ricky Ponting would have been proud of the shot. We ran three.

'Great over, Toby,' Jimbo said, patting me on the shoulder. 'Eight off it.' He turned to look at the scoreboard.

'Jimbo, there *is* a guy standing down there, isn't there?' Jimbo turned suddenly, detecting the desperation in my voice.

'Tell me where exactly,' he asked. A cold shiver suddenly ran up my spine. 'Toby, are you okay? What is it?'

'Oh my God, it's a Grubber,' I whispered, staring at the man. Now that he was closer I could see the off-white trousers and old-fashioned jumper. I'd been avoiding the plain truth. The man wasn't a groundsman or one of the coaches. He was on the ground, but why couldn't anyone see him? I looked at him more closely. He was of average height, with jet black hair that was slicked back, parted on either side, and he had a small moustache above his thin lips. He was glancing about nervously.

'A what?'

'Let's go, batters,' the umpire called. I went down to face the England spinner. The man had moved forward and was now only metres behind the fielder at wide mid-on.

'Hey!' I waved my bat in the fielder's direction, hoping he'd turn and see the guy just behind him. The England fielders stared at me.

'Are you ready?' the umpire called. I took the plunge.

'The guy out at mid-on,' I called, moving forward a few metres.

'What?' the fielder called. 'I'm allowed to field here, aren't I?'

'Let's get on with it,' called the umpire, shaking his head. I watched in amazement as the man approached the fielder, who was totally unaware that the Grubber was so close to him. I jerked my eyes back just in time as the English spinner tossed up a well-flighted delivery pitched on middle stump. Swinging my bat across the line of the ball I hoicked it out through mid-wicket.

Both the mid-on and the mid-wicket went scampering after the ball.

'Toby, run!' Jimbo called, already halfway down the pitch. We managed two on what should have been a three. Jimbo walked towards me.

'Toby, whatever it is, forget it, okay? We're in the middle of a bloody Ashes Test match.' We both turned as we heard an eerie gurgling sound coming from the fielder at mid-on. 'Geez, what's wrong with him?' said Jimbo.

The umpire and players ran over to the fielder who was lying on the ground, thrashing his arms and legs around. I noticed a couple of trainers sprinting onto the field.

'Freddy, what is it?' one of the England players shouted. It looked like Freddy was having some sort of convulsion. There was spit around his mouth, his eyes had that far away look and his jaw was rigid.

'Give him room, boys,' a trainer said, backing away himself. I looked around for the Grubber but there was no sign of him.

'Did anyone see a guy on the field?' I asked, exasperated. A few surprised faces turned to look at me. 'Well?'

'Toby, will you stop it about the guy? There's been no one on this field since lunch except the players and the two umps. What's got into you?' Jimbo stared at me, perhaps noticing the seriousness of my expression. He'd seen that expression before. 'Oh no,' he muttered, glancing around. 'You really did see someone? Toby?'

From behind Jimbo's right shoulder I spotted another of the Grubbers. This guy was wearing darker clothes and a cloth cap was slouched over his head. He was slowly walking towards the pitch.

'Jimbo, we've got to get everyone off the ground. There's another one coming.'

'Where? Show me exactly.'

'Look straight down from the right-hand edge of the scoreboard. He's walking towards us now.' I was trying to keep the panic from my voice. The English kid called Freddy was slowly getting to his feet.

'What happened?' one of his mates asked. Freddy shook his head. His eyes still looked vacant but he smiled and shrugged his shoulders.

'Don't know.' He spoke in a soft drawl. 'Cricket. Let's play cricket.' He clapped his hands together and moved back to his position. The trainers looked at each other and shrugged.

'Freddy, come in for a while and have a rest,' one of the trainers suggested, putting his hand on Freddy's shoulder. Freddy shrugged his hand away.

'Cricket,' he said again, firmly. 'Come along. I'm fine. I just fell and bumped my elbow,' he added, rubbing it.

'Bumped your head, more like,' Jimbo whispered. I didn't like it.

'Can you see him?'

'Toby, I can't see anyone.' The man had paused, eyeing us all warily.

'Keep an eye on him, Neville,' the other trainer said to the umpire. 'We'll come back out during drinks.'

My concentration was shot. What with watching another Grubber slowly advancing towards the wicket, listening to Freddy out at mid-on continually clapping his hands, and then trying to focus on the bowler, I did well to last three more deliveries. I was clean-bowled off the next.

I stood at the crease in a state of mild shock before trudging off. I was right in line with the Grubber who was making his slow advance, but I wasn't frightened. Instead, a wave of anger swept over me. I was handling the bowling okay. I was out on the MCG with Jimbo battling for Australia in a desperate partnership and then these Grubber spooks had to come and spoil it.

I glared at the figure as it moved towards me.

'Come on,' I challenged him, raising my bat. I was close enough now to see his face. It was a pale, ghostly colour — a lined, weathered face, with watery red eyes and the barest hint of a smile. The man looked old. Not as old as Jim, but way older than my dad.

Suddenly he raised his arms, pointing them towards me. I lifted my bat and swung it hard as he made his move. My bat swung right through him; there was no resistance at all.

'It's only a bloody game,' a fielder scoffed, jogging past me.

'Piss off!' I yelled, swinging my bat again.

'What did you say?' The fielder stopped, stunned.

'Not you,' I gasped. Then I ran as fast as I could as I felt an ice cold hand grab my arm. I flung it away, dropping my bat in the process. I got to the small gate and pushed through, bounding up the steps two at a time. It was only when I got to the top step that I turned around.

'No way,' I whispered, watching the man slowly pick himself up off the ground. It was the spookiest thing I'd ever seen. Maybe I had somehow connected with my bat.

'No!' I called, as a small kid dashed out onto the oval to collect my bat. The Grubber staggered, then fell back onto the grass.

'Here you go,' the kid said, handing me the bat. 'Can I have your autograph?'

'What?'

'Your autograph.' I glanced at the scoreboard. 6–78. Pathetic. We were in real strife.

'Later,' I mumbled. I needed Jim and I needed him fast. Before the Grubber found another fielder. Or Jimbo. Because I was certain now that somehow the Grubber had taken over Freddy; got to him in some way. Was Freddy now a Grubber?

3 William and the Amazing Glass Tube

Saturday — afternoon

'What on earth did you think you were doing out there?' Marty glared at me.

'Marty, I can't explain now,' I said, looking him in the eye. He must have noticed the expression of anguish on my face because his tone softened.

'Listen, Toby. There was an old guy called Jim in here before ...'

'Jim? Where is he now?'

'Beats me.'

'How long ago?' I was wondering if he'd seen the last half hour.

'Just after lunch. Toby, go and speak to him. You are both stressed about something.' Marty raised his hands in a sign of surrender. 'When you get yourself back here, be ready to play some cricket, okay?'

'Thanks, Marty. Don't worry. As long as Jimbo's batting, we're a chance.'

We both turned as a loud shout erupted from the field. Marty groaned.

'It's a shame there's no such thing as last man's tucker in Ashes Tests.'

Grabbing a drink from the fridge at the back of the players' viewing room I headed to the library.

'Hi, David,' I called out to the librarian. 'Have you ... Jim!' The two of them were standing in front of the MCC library's complete set of *Wisden*s. 'Jim, we have to talk.'

'Here we are,' David said, opening an ancient-looking *Wisden*. 'Stan Northington. Played his last Test match at the MCG on 3 March 1937.'

'Well done, David,' said Jim. 'Keep looking, will you? I can't explain now but I shall need you to find me any other English players who played their last Test matches here. Probably pre-war only.' The MCC librarian's eyes lit up.

'It could take some time.'

'And time is something we don't have,' Jim muttered. He rested a hand on my shoulder. 'Toby, I'm sorry about your downfall.'

'Downfall?'

'Your dismissal. Being bowled like that.'

'You saw?'

Jim's eyes sparkled softly. 'In a manner of speaking. Come along; we have to talk. I need you to take me somewhere.' I followed Jim into David's office. 'Don't worry, Toby. I have spoken to young Marty.' Jim picked up an old *Wisden* from David's table. He looked at me, his face tinged with sadness. 'Toby, the time I have feared for so many years might have finally arrived. I need your help; cricket needs your help. I don't think I can do this alone.'

Jim walked out of the office, still holding the *Wisden*. Suddenly he was moving quickly and I was struggling to keep up with him.

'Is it Father Time?' I asked, almost jogging alongside him. Jim paused.

'Toby, I am going to do something that I hoped I would never have to do. At least not in these circumstances.' We paused outside the door to the Committee Room; the room that led to the special Sanctum Room where we'd met the Cricket Lord who'd helped cure Ally.

'The Sanctum?' I breathed, following Jim into the kitchen. 'But what . . .'

Jim held up a hand.

'Trust me, Toby.' Jim held the cover of the *Wisden* up to the small window in the kitchen and I heard the sound of something shifting. You would never have known the window was part of a small door, built into the wall. I moved uneasily, remembering who I had encountered the last time I was here. Jim must have sensed my nervousness; he squeezed my shoulder.

'It's all right, Toby. We're expected.' The door clicked and Jim pushed it open. I followed him into the Sanctum. It was a room that defied logic; it was just not physically possible that such a large room could exist here in the middle of the MCG Members Stand. 'Come along, Toby,' Jim said softly.

'I feared this moment was nigh,' a deep voice called from the shadows ahead of us. A tall man in faded white cricket clothes and a strange coloured cap stepped forward, his hand outstretched towards Jim. A blue and red striped jacket hung limply from his thin frame. They shook hands. 'Toby Jones,' he said, turning to me. I shook his hand. 'I have heard so much about you, young fellow. And given that it's still more than 100 years before you're born, I think that's quite something, don't you?'

'Jim? What year is this?'

'Toby, we are a long way back. It's 1883, though the *Wisden Cricketer's Almanack* is already nearly twenty years old.' Jim's voice suddenly changed. 'Toby, look at me.' The two men stood over me.

'W-what is it?' I asked.

'The time has come, Toby, for you to be appointed as a Cricket Lord. We are faced with perhaps the biggest ...' Jim started to explain.

'Toby, Jim's time with you is over. He has been called to serve ...' the other man interrupted.

'William!' Jim snapped, frowning.

'You said so yourself, Jim. The boy is wise enough even at his tender age to know.'

'Hey! I'm in the middle of a Test match against England at the MCG,' I protested.

'And the best is yet to come,' William laughed, patting me on the shoulder. 'That second ball of your third over will be talked about for years.'

'William, please!' admonished Jim.

'What ball? What happened?' I asked.

'Enough of this, you two. William, see to Toby's stump,' Jim ordered. William sighed and headed over to an old-looking table covered with an assortment of strange objects. 'Toby, as you know, the situation is not good.'

'The Grubbers?' I queried.

'The Grubbers, yes. They are leaving the Timeless Cricket Match and returning to various places in time and space, as you saw. Each is returning to the venue of their last cricket match,' Jim explained.

'You saw the guy on the field? The one who approached the England fielder?' I asked.

'Yes,' Jim said sadly.

'Will he be all right?'

'That, dear Toby, depends very much on you. The boy has had his soul taken over by the Grubber. That's what I was talking about to David in the library. It helps if we can identify him and thus talk to him. All we know is that the Grubber who walked onto the field would have played his last Test match at the MCG.'

'But that could be anyone.'

'Well, not exactly anyone. His cricket clothes narrow the search somewhat.' I thought of the old creams and heavy jumper he was wearing. I vaguely recalled a blue 'V', but I didn't remember any logos or numbers on it.

'Was he from England?'

'Yes, I believe so. And probably pre-war too. But it confirms my suspicions. The Grubbers are leaving; the Timeless Cricket Match is under threat and if the game stops, of course the scoring stops.'

'Father Time will escape from the scoreboard?' I asked, keeping one eye on William who was lifting up a long, glass cylinder.

'I can't imagine the havoc he could cause. That's why you're here, Toby. I'm afraid you're going to have to take up the fight while I monitor what's happening at the Timeless Match.'

'What's going to happen here?' I looked around the vast chamber we were standing in. Apart from the old wooden table and the assortment of cricket objects on it, the room was bare.

'Toby, you are going to become a Cricket Lord. This is not a decision I take lightly but the Grubbers leaving the Timeless Cricket Match is a potentially calamitous situation. We need all the help we can get.'

'Ready, Jim,' William called from the table.

'Come along, Toby. I think you will enjoy this.' I followed Jim to the table. 'But, William, we don't have much time. Toby has a cricket match to get back to.'

'Very well.' William pushed a tall glass jar across the table towards me. Thin wisps of white smoke swirled inside it. 'Toby, place both your hands on the jar and look into it carefully.' The coldness of the glass surprised me but I held on all the same and stared at the smoke billowing around. As I watched, it seemed to be getting thicker.

'What's supposed to happen?'

'You'll see, Toby. You'll see,' said Jim. For a minute I stood there, my hands slowly warming, but nothing inside the tall glass cylinder changed.

'Jim, are you sure?' I heard William whisper.

'Sure about ...' My fingers started to tingle. There was a smell of burning in the room and I immediately thought of the stumps I'd seen last time I was here. Each Cricket Lord had a partly burnt stump, made from a special willow tree, signifying that they were a Cricket Lord. I didn't take my hands from the jar. Suddenly the smoke inside the jar cleared. I gasped in awe as a little village green materialised inside the glass. There were trees and cows and a group of men walking out onto a clearing. I couldn't make out a pitch or a scoreboard. A bowler was bowling underarm.

'Good Lord,' I heard William breathe, standing next to me. 'He's predating *Wisdens*.' I glanced at Jim quickly.

'Predating, Toby. You're looking at cricket events from before 1863. Before *Wisdens*.'

'This is remarkable,' said William.

'I told you he was special,' Jim said, softly. 'Don't take your hands from the glass, Toby. Hang on for the ride of your life.'

The scene quickly changed to a cobbled street with a group of boys playing a game. But as soon as that scene became clear inside the glass it also disappeared, and suddenly I was watching an old-fashioned looking lady playing cricket in a beautiful garden. She was bowling a strange style of side-arm on account of her wide dress. I don't know how I knew this. The people close by her were talking excitedly, gesticulating with their arms and imitating her strange bowling action. But the image quickly dissolved again and a new picture materialised.

Just a remnant of thin white smoke hovered over the constantly changing scenes. Men wearing tall black hats with huge moustaches and long beards changed to images of other old cricketers batting, bowling and fielding at different grounds from around the world.

The slide show of moving images changed at an increasingly faster rate. I recognised the flashing blade of Don Bradman hitting a cracking cover drive; saw a crowd of fielders hovering around a batsman on a dark and patchy wicket. I watched in amazement as wickets tumbled, boundaries were scored and catches taken.

Now the scenes were flashing by too quickly for me to recognise any person or event.

'Keep your hands on the glass, Toby Jones,' William said. It was becoming more difficult to focus on the flashing images. I thought I recognised the enormous stands of the MCG, but maybe not. Inside the glass soon became a blur of white and green. I could feel my hands warming rapidly. 'Hands, Toby.' It was as if William knew that it was starting to get uncomfortable.

I noticed a flash of yellow followed by the unmistakable sight of black words and numbers swirling around in a mixture of white. I stole a brief look at Jim.

'Hold on, Toby,' he whispered. 'It's nearly done.'

My hands prickled with the heat from the glass. It was getting too hot, I thought, and panic swept through me as my arms twitched. I felt droplets of sweat tickle my forehead and I tried to focus on that rather than on the searing pain in my hands.

Finally, just when I thought I'd have to let go, the white fog descended from the top of the jar, quickly smothering the latest image of the World Cup trophy, and the glass started to cool again.

'It's done, Toby. Let go and take hold of these two items,' William said, holding out a stump and a cricket ball. One end of the stump was smouldering and I realised that this was the source of the sweet aroma that filled the air. The ball felt good in my hand. Then Jim began talking in a quiet voice.

> 'Now should there come a time one day
> When the ghosts of watchers find a way
> To leave forever the Timeless Match
> Then with the Lord's ball take the catch

Four simple words you then must shout,
Tell the host, "You've been caught out!"'

The words had barely left his lips when I experienced an overwhelming feeling of calm and ease; I had never felt more relaxed in my life. It was a sensation of floating free, high above the glass tube and the table, Jim and William, the room and the MCG; drifting above the city itself. Moving further and further away.

'Remarkable,' I heard William say quietly. Opening my eyes again I waited a few moments for the room to come into focus.

'I told you.' Jim held his hand out to me.

'Am I a Cricket Lord?'

'My favourite part,' William chuckled, gently taking the stump from my hand. 'Let's see if the cricket law and knowledge is yours.' I offered him the ball too. 'Oh no, Toby. That, my friend, is something you don't want to ever let go. And mind you, don't play cricket with it either. Whatever you wish the ball to do, it will!'

'Please, William. All that I can explain some other time.' Jim looked at me. 'Toby, I recited the words of the sixth verse of the poem to you. Can you recite them back to me?' I closed my eyes and spoke the words. I knew them somehow, though I'd made no conscious effort to try and remember the verse.

'How did that happen?' I asked, looking from Jim to William. Jim smiled.

'Just five questions, William. And then we must be off.'

'Very well,' William said, his voice bright and cheerful. He seemed to be enjoying the ceremony heaps. William pressed his hands together, his fingertips touching his lips. 'Toby, how many runs did Viv Richards make in the first Test match against England during the West Indies' 1976 tour of England?'

'232,' I replied. I glanced at Jim, wondering whether he'd whispered the number to me. Like the poem, the answer had just popped into my head. 'Is that right?'

'Yes,' William smiled.

'B-but . . .'

'Can you tell me anything about his innings?'

I stared at William, suddenly panicking. I didn't know the first thing about his innings. I'd heard of Viv Richards, but that's all.

'Relax, Toby,' Jim said, smiling. 'It can be a little daunting to begin with — all this cricket knowledge you have suddenly gained.' I closed my eyes, channelling my mind onto Viv Richards and his score. In a flash the answer was as clear as the table in front of me.

'He had a partnership of 303 with Alvin Kallicharran. It was a brilliant innings. He hit 36 runs off his last 13 balls before being caught by Tony Greig on the boundary line.'

'Where was he caught, Toby?' William asked, his eyes never leaving my face.

'Long off.'

'I think that proves things, don't you, William?' Jim was in a hurry to get me back to the game. But William held up a hand.

'Let's go back a little in time, Toby. Who made 193 for Australia?'

'Warren Bardsley, Lord's, the second Test against England, 1926.' William stared at me, a smile slowly spreading across his old, wrinkled face. 'Not out,' I added.

'It is done,' he said, looking over at Jim and nodding. 'He is indeed a talent. I would so like to question him further, Jim. He might even attain your lofty standards.'

'I've no doubt about that at all, William. But another time, perhaps.' Jim was already halfway to the door.

'Young Toby,' William whispered, resting his hand on my arm. I looked into his blue eyes. 'Well done, boy. On many counts, well done!'

'Thanks.'

'Toby, don't ever despair of the knowledge you have suddenly gained. It is a gift to inspire, not a burden to bear. Remember that.'

'I will.' I paused for a moment, letting his words sink in, and then turned and ran, catching up with Jim. When I glanced back, William and the table were almost too far away to see, tiny specks in the distance.

'Toby,' Jim said, pausing at the door. 'I know there is much to explain but I will only say this. Treasure the cricket ball here as if your life depended on it. It is more powerful even than the scorecard.'

'Where's your cricket ball?' I asked.

'You have held it in your hand, Toby.'

'Really? When?'

'In your back garden. We used to play cricket with it!'

'But you never told me.' Jim looked at me and smiled.

'I know,' he replied.

4 Return to the Timeless Cricket Match

Saturday — afternoon

'Jim, it's raining!' I cried, glancing at the scoreboard behind me as I followed him towards the library. We were 9–107 and still in strife.

'Toby, I need you to take me to the Timeless Cricket Match. Now that you're a Cricket Lord there's a very simple way of doing it.'

'Jim,' David called, looking up from a huge pile of *Wisden*s spread across the table he was sitting at.

Jim picked up one of the *Wisden*s and marched across to David's small office. 'Remarkably easy, as you will see,' he said, closing the door behind us.

'But you want me to come too?'

'Just to carry me there,' said Jim, opening up the *Wisden*. He didn't appear to be paying too much attention to where he was actually looking. I watched his old fingers quickly turn the pages.

'What are you looking for?' I asked.

'Perhaps the most common and talked about cricket score of them all,' he said. 'Ah, here we are. Nought, or, as this generation likes to call it, a duck.' Jim reached out and took my hand. 'Toby, this won't take ...'

David's office disappeared and instead of looking at a painted wall I was suddenly staring at a copse of bent and gnarly looking trees. I shivered, the coldness of the place pressing in.

'Thank you, Toby. That ...'

'Jim!' I shouted, as a ghostly form swooped down towards us. In a flash Jim had spun around and hurled something in its direction. Its face twisted in pain and it cried out as the cricket ball from Jim's pocket struck it.

'A Grubber,' Jim grunted, walking towards his ball. The Grubber was lying on the ground, wheezing and choking. 'Time for you to leave, Toby. This is my battleground. Yours is back at the MCG playing cricket.'

I didn't like the sound of the word battleground.

'Jim, let me just stay with you for a while.' I swung to my right just in time to see another Grubber moving quickly towards us, his face grim and determined. He was like a zombie. I reached into my pocket and hurled the ball at it. To my astonishment the Grubber kept on coming, barely flinching.

As the Grubber raised its arms Jim threw his ball again, this time connecting with it right on the chest.

I turned away as a plume of smoke rose from the place where the ball had connected.

'Toby, enough!' Jim barked, turning on me. 'Leave at once.'

'But, Jim,' I cried, glancing about. 'I can't leave you here. What if a whole lot come at you? You've only got the one ball.'

'Toby, I can and will look after myself.' His voice softened as I felt my face redden. 'They only ever attack alone; rarely in pairs, unless they sense weakness.' He sighed, forcing his lips into a smile. 'My time is here and now; yours is not.' He reached out his arms. 'You must go, Toby.'

'W-why didn't my cricket ball work?'

'The four words from the last verse, Toby. You forgot to say them or even think them.' He squeezed my shoulders. 'Goodbye, my boy.'

I watched him follow a narrow path towards a clump of twisted and ghostly looking trees. He didn't look back. Just as he was about to disappear over a rise, another Grubber suddenly appeared on the path behind him.

'Jim!' I shrieked, sprinting towards him. Jim didn't appear to have heard me, nor had he noticed the Grubber just metres behind him.

'You've been caught out!' I shrieked, hurling the ball in the direction of the Grubber. It caught him smack in the middle of his back. His body twisted in agony and he fell to the ground, a wisp of brown smoke slowly curling up from the spot where the ball had connected.

To my astonishment, Jim kept on walking as if nothing had happened. Collecting the cricket ball I cautiously moved further along the track, keeping a lookout for any more Grubbers.

I got to the rise where I had last seen Jim and looked out over the cricket ground, only 60 metres away. The game had paused; the old players were standing around in groups. I looked at the umpire, who was pointing towards an old pavilion. There was no sign of Jim. The Grubber I had stopped had got to his knees and was now crawling off in another direction.

There appeared to be only a sprinkling of people watching the play. Vast spaces of emptiness surrounded the oval with the occasional Grubber still moving about down near the fence. It seemed that not all of the Grubbers were unfriendly, as some preferred to stay close to the oval and the cricket being played out in the middle, rather than moving to attack.

Then I glanced up at the scoreboard. I shivered at the thought that Father Time might be locked away behind its huge wooden face. The score read 8–379. As I stared up at the enormous wooden structure, I noticed one of the numbers alongside a bowler's name slowly change. For a brief moment I thought I could see inside as a '7' disappeared and was replaced by a '0'.

Was the scoreboard returning to a wall of zeroes, as Jim had predicted would happen if the Timeless Cricket Match ended?

A voice called from the field. The players had returned to their positions and one of them was clapping. The bowler gazed around the field, nodded once then slowly made his way in to the crease.

Taking one more look at the scoreboard I backed away, reciting the first two lines of the poem. I felt a cool breeze lightly brush my cheeks as I made the trip back to my time. It happened so quickly I barely had a chance to register the actual travel itself.

Just as I had before, I was going to have to trust Jim. Maybe he was now in a special place with other Cricket Lords. It didn't feel right to leave him there, but there was nothing else I could do.

'Come on, Toby!' Jimbo called, as I raced back towards the players' room. The team was heading out onto the ground in single file. 'Look!' I followed Jimbo's gaze.

'The lights!' I cried, gawping at the enormous array of bright, white lights beaming down onto the ground.

'Toby!' Marty yelled at me. I stopped suddenly.

'Marty, I can explain.' Actually, I had no hope of explaining.

'Toby, I've just been talking with Brian Casboult.' Marty was waiting for some sort of reaction, but I had no idea who he was talking about.

'Yeah?' Maybe this Brian Casboult was the match official or something. Had I been disqualified from the game for not being here?

'Brian Casboult, the chief executive of the Melbourne Cricket Ground.'

'Oh.' I *had* been dumped.

'He said that you are to have full access to any person and any place in the entire ground.'

'He did?' Marty nodded. 'Does that mean I'm good to go?' This time Marty grinned. 'Good as gold. I've got no idea what you and that old guy ...'

'That's Jim.'

'Yeah. I've got no idea what you and Jim are up to, but right now we need a few wickets. You heard of the expression of having your back to the wall?' I nodded, keen to join the rest of the team out on the ground. 'Well, this is the Wall of China, Toby.'

'I'm going to walk that one day,' I smiled, catching the green cap that Marty finally flung in my direction. I pulled the ball out of my pocket to put in my bag.

'You're not nicking balls, are you?' Marty said, holding out his hand for it.

'Oh, n-no, um, this is mine,' I said, trying to sound relaxed. 'It's got sentimental value.' I stashed it deep inside my kit.

'Fair enough,' he grinned. 'Go climb that wall, Toby Jones.'

5 Perfect Conditions

We had been dismissed for 109 and things didn't get any better at the start of England's innings. Scott bowled three no balls in his first two overs, but it was his third no ball that had us all reeling.

The England opener had taken a hefty swipe and the ball caught a thick outside edge and flew to Sean in the gully.

'Yeeeeeeessssss!' Scott roared, charging down the pitch and thrusting his arm out towards the dressing room. He was 'politely' telling the batter where he should be heading. But the batter stood his ground, before finally moving a few paces backwards as Scott got close to him.

'Next time, Scott,' Jimbo called, clapping his hands.

'What?' Scott swore and kicked out with his foot, making a decent scrape mark in the pitch down near the batter. My heart sank as the two umpires converged. They called over Sean and then Scott.

Jimbo, Cam and I pressed in closer to hear what was being said but it was over in moments. One of the umpires pulled out his walkie talkie and the next moment Scott had snatched his cap and was storming off the field. He'd been sent off for scuffing the pitch, but I'm sure his swearing had helped the umpires come to their decision.

'We're not allowed a twelfth man either,' Sean said, glaring at Scott's back. After the groundsman had repaired the pitch as best he could, we settled back in to the task.

England had spanked 23 runs off our first four overs and we were in deep trouble. And then it suddenly got worse. Heaps worse.

Just after delivering the first ball of his third over, Greg, our fastest bowler, crashed to the ground, clutching his right ankle. We raced in from everywhere but I knew straight away it wasn't good. Two trainers finally managed to haul him to his feet and we watched, forlorn, as he hobbled off the field.

'I assume we get a twelfth man this time?' Jaimi, our other pace bowler, said.

'Come on, guys,' said Sean. 'We're not out of this.'

'Our two best bowlers are off,' said Wesley, our keeper, 'we've scored just over 100 runs and they're none for 23 after four overs. Give it a break, Sean.'

I turned on Wesley and scowled. 'Sean's right.' I looked past him to a spot in the Southern Stand. It was almost exactly where I'd sat and watched Andrew Symonds make his first Test hundred against England. 'Hey, remember the Ashes Test here that we won by an innings and 99 runs? Andrew Symonds came out to bat with the score at 5 for 84? They were down then. And what did Symonds do? He didn't even know the score as he walked out. He knew that if he thought about it too much, he'd get edgy, grip the bat too hard, get all tense. So he just played his natural game and got on with it.'

'And scored 150-plus runs,' Sean said, nodding.

'Come on, guys. We fight this one out to the end.'

'Bloody oath we do,' Jimbo said, nodding at me. We broke up, but I paused as Sean called my name.

'Who shall I bowl?' he asked, quietly.

'I reckon give Barton Rivers a go,' I said. 'Surprise them a bit.'

'And he might do something with that footmark,' Sean added, grinning. I'd had exactly the same thought myself.

I bowled the final five deliveries of Greg's over, all away swingers and only one played at. It connected with the middle of his bat.

We got our breakthrough in the next over when Barton enticed the batter to sweep. But it collected a top edge. I ran around from my position at backward square leg about 10 metres and took a comfortable catch.

A ripple of applause erupted from the crowd scattered around the ground and enjoying the sun which had finally broken through.

'How long is Scott off for?' I asked Sean as he passed me the ball for my second over.

'That's now in the hands of the two coaches,' he said.

'What, Marty and the English coach?' Sean nodded.

My next over was much like the first, with the batter only having to play at a couple. The last ball fizzed over his off-stump.

'Good watching, Seb,' the non-striker called out. I glared at the opener.

'Mate, what's he brought a bat out for?'

'You'll probably find out next over,' he said, and wandered off down the pitch. I grinned at his back.

I had the first drop on strike for my third over. Yet again he let the first ball go. I was feeling good; the rhythm was there and my run-up felt smooth. I came in a bit closer to the umpire with the next ball. It started outside off-stump but, unlike all the previous balls, swung the other way viciously, smashing into the guy's off-stump. What was even more satisfying was that he'd shouldered arms, raising his bat high in the air, assuming it was going to easily miss off-stump.

I didn't look at the non-striker. I reckoned that actions spoke louder than words anyway.

'Oh my God!' I gasped as I suddenly recalled what William had said.

'What is it, Toby?' Jimbo asked, looking concerned. It was only when I was looking at the replay on the scoreboard that I'd remembered.

'The second ball of your third over,' I said quietly to myself. Looking over towards our dressing rooms I noticed Marty and another man. It looked like they were deep in conversation. I turned to Jimbo and grinned.

'I'll explain later,' I told him, taking the ball from Sean and heading back.

'Hey, it's that weird guy,' one of the players said. 'He's not wearing a helmet either.' I turned again and watched Freddy approach the wicket. Was I imagining it or was there a glint in his eye? There was a look about him that was all determination and hardness. Our eyes met. He stared at me with an intensity I'd never encountered on a cricket field before.

My first ball to him was just short of a length, outside off-stump. He rocked back and carved it out through point. I watched the ball speed across the turf, ricochet off the rope and crash hard into the hoardings beyond the rope. It rebounded 20 metres back onto the field.

Jaimi out at mid-off swore under his breath. 'What's his bat made out of?' he said, tossing me the ball. I shrugged.

'He found the sweet spot all right.' I pitched the next ball fuller. Freddy was on it in a flash, belting it along the ground to Jaimi's left. The ball was past Jaimi before he'd even responded to the shot. The sound of ball hitting bat was like the crack of a whip echoing around the ground.

The last two balls were on line and he pushed them back along the pitch.

'I'd have him in my team,' Jimbo grinned, jogging past me at the end of the over.

'Geez yeah.'

'I reckon the Poms would have him in their *senior* Test team,' he added. I stopped dead. Jimbo kept on going.

'Jimbo?'

'Come on, Toby!' Sean called, clapping his hands. I jogged quickly to my position, never taking my eyes off Freddy, who was standing nonchalantly at the non-striker's end, leaning on his bat.

Was it Freddy batting, or was it a Grubber? A former Test cricketer, returned to the ground he last played on? He was sure batting like a Test player.

'Toby!' I heard my name yelled. The ball had ballooned out towards me. Too late I ran back, getting to it on the first bounce. I hurled it back at Wesley in disgust. My mind had been completely elsewhere and we'd just missed out on a massive chance to get a third wicket. Kicking the ground in disgust, I went back to my position.

'Sorry, Barton,' I called. He gave me a little wave. We gathered together for the drinks break.

'Hey!' I spun around.

'Georgie! What are you doing out here?'

'Marty, your coach, is so nice. He let me help the twelfth man bring out the drinks. Neat, huh?'

But I didn't get much time to talk to her. Sean

called Jimbo and me back to the group for another chat.

I was determined to make amends in my next over. I bowled Freddy a bouncer. Helmet, or no helmet; I didn't care. The ball was spearing towards his head and for a frightening moment I thought he was going to collect it on the scone, but in the last instant, he flashed his bat across his face.

Crack! The ball flew away over backward square leg for a massive six. It was a great result for him but I wasn't convinced by the shot and he knew it.

'Sean, can I have another one behind square leg?' I called. He took out a slip. Taking a deep breath, I charged in again. But instead of the expected short ball I bowled a fuller, slower ball. Freddy had anticipated the bouncer and already moved back towards his stumps. He jammed his bat down on the ball when he realised where it had pitched but missed it completely. The ball cannoned into his back pad.

'Howzzatt!' I screamed, staring at the umpire. He didn't move. I'd caught him plumb on the crease, dead in front. Finally, after what seemed like an eternity, the umpire slowly raised his arm, his right index pointing to the sky. 'Yeeeeeeeeeeeees!' I screeched, charging down the pitch. The others rushed in.

'I'm really sorry about that pathetic effort, last over,' I said again, this time in front of the whole team.

'Yeah, well you looked like you were in another world,' Sean grinned. I immediately thought of Jim, literally in another world. 'But he's the one we wanted.' We all watched the replay.

'3–44. Game on, Jones.' Jimbo slapped me on the back.

'Too right.'

I took another four wickets as the England team slumped to be all out for 122. They had a slender lead of only 13 runs.

'Quick runs and we do it all again,' Sean said, as we strode off the ground, our confidence restored.

'Except for that Freddy bloke,' Wesley muttered, darkly.

'Hey, Wesley. Lighten up. We got him out once. We can get him out again.'

I silently agreed with Sean, but I was thinking of a completely different way of getting him out.

6 The Chase for Freddy Barnes

Saturday — afternoon

Jim hadn't said whether my cricket ball would work against a Grubber that had possessed someone, or what would happen to the possessed person themselves, but I was almost certain that Freddy had been somehow taken over by the Grubber Jim had first seen on the oval earlier in the day.

I wasn't sure exactly what I was going to do when I confronted Freddy, but I needed my cricket ball and I needed to find him before he went back out onto the ground.

'Guys, that was a great effort ...' said Marty.

'Marty, my cricket ball?' I interrupted, rummaging through my kit. Marty glared at me, then must have remembered what Brian Casboult had said. But I felt stupid suddenly and apologised. 'Sorry, Marty. Go on.' I buried my head in my bag to hide my embarrassment.

What had got into me? Surely another hour or so wasn't going to matter too much? Or would every minute count for Freddy? Maybe even now his personality had been taken over so completely that he couldn't be saved.

Marty finished his speech and came over to me.

'I'm sorry, Marty,' I began, but he held up a hand.

'No, that's all right. Listen, I think one of the kids might have been rummaging through your bag. There was stuff everywhere. I put all the balls over there somewhere,' he said, pointing vaguely to a spot beneath the window. 'There was a box there.' I felt a wave of panic.

'Over where, Marty?' I said, trying to stay calm.

'Over ... Hey! Oh, maybe Tom took the box down to the nets. You can go and throw a few at our openers.'

'Who was going through my kit, and why?' I fumed under my breath, racing down to the indoor nets.

'Toby, grab a couple of balls and throw a few at Cam, would you?' Tom called, as I entered the nets area.

'Actually I was ...' I stopped mid-sentence as I watched Scott send down a whopping outswinger to Jimbo.

'Hey, Temple, that's four in a row you've missed!' Scott laughed, catching the ball Jimbo tossed back to him. I knew straight away that Scott had my cricket ball. I closed my eyes briefly. How typical! He looked in my direction and smirked.

'You're on the same side, Scott,' I lashed out, suddenly angry. 'Trying to build *up* his confidence before he goes out to bat, not get him out.'

'Piss off, Jones. You're talking out of your backside. This is much better preparation than bowling up your pathetic little half-volleys.' He took a step towards me. 'That's not what they're going to bowl out there!' He pointed in the general direction of the ground. 'It's a bloody Test match, not some little kiddy game in a park.'

'Yeah? It was too big an event for you to keep your cool, Scott. Great job you did for the team.' I held my ground, knowing I'd gone too far. We stood there, both breathing hard, toe to toe.

'Toby, just toss me a couple out here, would you?' Jimbo called. 'Or someone.'

'Give me the ball, Scott,' I said, holding out my hand.

'No way, Jones. Not this one. It reverse swings a mile.' Scott had apparently forgotten my outburst, or chosen to ignore my words. Perhaps he needed his ego stroked. 'Watch this.' He trotted back a few paces, turned and jogged in. The ball he bowled swung viciously from outside Jimbo's off-stump, clipping him on the pads and crashing into the net behind. Was he wishing the ball to swing like that? Surely not.

'Here, Jimbo!' I called, sticking up my right hand and walking down the wicket towards him. I felt a shove from behind.

'No way, Jones,' Scott sneered, pushing me out of the way as Jimbo tossed the ball towards us. 'This is my ball, mate.'

'You ready, Jimbo?' someone called from the doorway. I shrugged my shoulders at Jimbo, wished him good luck and set off after Scott.

'Scott, wait up!' I shouted. He'd gone into the far net. 'Can I just take a look at that ball?'

'Why?'

'Well actually, it's my ball.' Scott glared at me and I realised how pathetic I sounded. I wasn't about to tell him about the Cricket Lords and what the ball could actually do. 'Um, it was a gift and it's just special, that's all.'

'I don't see anything on it that tells me it's your ball, Jones.'

'Everything okay there?' Tom, one of the coaches, called, as he packed up the other balls and equipment.

'All good,' I replied, never taking my eyes off the ball. I sighed. 'Okay, Scott. I'll play you for it.'

'What do you mean?' He was interested, I could tell.

'Two overs each. No protection for the batter. Indoor cricket scoring plus any runs you can make.'

'And I get to use this ball?'

'As long as I get to use it too. And the winner gets the ball.'

'Forever?' A small grin slowly broke out on his face. I nodded. 'Toss you to bat first. Tom?' he called, not even turning around. 'Can you umpire this game for us?' Tom paused by the door.

'Sure, explain the rules,' he said, walking towards us.

I won the toss and chose to bat.

'Yeah, well that suits me,' Scott laughed. 'I was going to bowl anyway.'

'Toby, you'll need to put on a helmet and a box,' said Tom, as I walked into the net with nothing but my bat.

'No way,' Scott cried. 'That's what we agreed on.'

'Then you shouldn't have asked me to umpire. Do you think I'm that stupid to let either of you face up to the other without at least some protection? Now, I know there's no love lost between you, which is a real shame as you're two of the most talented cricketers we've had at these camps.'

'We agreed . . .'

'Scott, wait for Toby to put on his gear or get out of here,' said Tom. I grabbed a box, slammed on a helmet and took guard.

'Twelve balls only,' Tom said, taking up position at the bowler's end. 'And you want lbw?'

'Not for the first 12 balls,' I grinned. Tom winked.

'Hang on,' Scott bellowed. 'That's not fair.' I rolled my eyes.

'Joking!'

I knew Scott was thinking swing, reverse or otherwise. Hopefully that's all I would have to try and play for. Expecting a big inswinger first up, I eased back, conscious of keeping my bat and pad as close together as possible. But instead, he bowled a huge outswinger. I missed it by a mile.

I was rapped on the pads three times with his next five balls, but each was swinging too much for Tom to give the lbw decision.

'It's beautiful bowling, Scott,' Tom called. A couple of coaches and players had wandered in to watch. I noticed Tom glance up above me. Two men wearing ties and jackets were sitting in the coaching booth on the next level.

I ran a single off the next ball and edged his eighth delivery into the back net. Scott yelled his appeal but it had travelled along the ground. Before he realised, I had snuck another two runs.

Four balls to go. Should I go for the slog and try and add some valuable runs but also risk a five-run penalty for getting out? Or should I try and sneak a couple more ones and twos?

Moving slightly out of my crease, I settled over my bat and waited. He dug the next ball in short. No time to swing, I hoped, getting quickly inside the line and belting it into the side netting. I set off for a single, and turned it into another two as Scott fumbled with the ball in the netting. He hurled it at the stumps but I'd made my ground. I snuck yet another single. I had now scored eight runs. I managed another two runs off his next two deliveries but was clean-bowled by a massively swinging ball on his last. Ten runs had suddenly turned into five runs in the space of one ball.

'Scott!' I yelled, rushing towards him. He had placed the ball on the ground, and while Tom's attention was diverted, I was convinced he was about to tread on it. His spikes would have made a mess of the ball. He looked up all innocent.

'What?' he glared at me, then picked up the ball and hurled it at me.

'Stop!' I yelled, staring in horror as the ball headed for my face. I threw up a hand, more in self-defence than in an attempt to catch it. But I needn't have bothered. To my utter amazement, the ball hung in the air, frozen in front of my face. I quickly snatched the ball, pretending nothing had happened, and desperately hoping that none of the bystanders had seen it either.

'What the —?' Scott began, his mouth open.

'What?' I eyed him suspiciously. 'Just good reflexes, that's all.'

'No, that ball . . .'

'Come on, Scott. We should be out there watching the game.' I walked past him, and called to Tom, who was chatting with a couple of guys near the doorway. The two men upstairs had left the booth. Perhaps that was a good thing.

Scott took his time getting himself organised, but finally after a stern word from Tom, who probably thought we should also be back upstairs with the team, he finally settled over his bat.

'Hit the stumps,' I whispered softly, the ball near my mouth. It tingled and felt good in my hand; bright white stitching and a deep cherry red colour with one side so shiny I could almost see my reflection. Scott's two overs with the ball hadn't dulled the shine at all.

The ball swung back sharply from outside Scott's off-stump, deflecting off the inside edge of his bat and cannoning into the stumps. Scott swore loudly, swinging his bat at the stumps. Kicking the ball back to me, Scott adjusted his helmet.

'I can't see out of this,' he snapped. I didn't reply.

'Find the edge of the bat,' I said quietly, as I walked back to the top of my mark. The next ball swung hard again, crashing into Scott's pads. I didn't detect a nick but Scott looked anxiously at Tom before once again kicking the ball in my direction.

'Why on earth didn't you appeal?' Tom asked, as I brushed past him.

'He hit it, didn't he?'

Tom raised an eyebrow. 'Did he? I'd make a hopeless umpire.'

I bowled Scott out twice more. I sensed his final score of minus four could have been a lot worse. But I'd decided that he was still a part of the Aussie team and would be a better player if his confidence wasn't shredded by being dismissed by Toby Jones six times in two overs.

Scott threw me the ball, still muttering about the helmet. It seemed a perfect fit to me.

'Thanks, Tom,' I said, trying to shove the ball into my pocket.

'You were playing for that?' Tom asked, holding out a hand for the ball. I tossed it to him.

'It has special value to me,' I said, watching him nervously as he turned the ball over in his hand.

'It talks, Toby,' he grinned, lobbing it back to me. 'Fast bowlers love a ball that talks.'

'You can say that again.' I smiled to myself.

We'd made another solid start with Jimbo and Cam both on 13 not out. I noticed that Jaimi Clayton, our number eight, had the pads on.

'Nightwatchman?' I asked, sitting down next to him. He nodded, not taking his eyes off the play. A nightwatchman is used near the end of the day's play when you need to protect your main batters. If a wicket falls, the captain can choose to send in one of the bowlers. Jaimi was the designated nightwatchman.

Freddy was standing at second slip, his hands on his hips. I watched him carefully during the last few overs of the day, looking for any sign that he might be behaving a bit differently from how he should be, but there was nothing about him that made him stand out from the rest of his team.

He walked slowly between the change of overs, often looking up into the stands and at the scoreboard. But then, we all did that. It wasn't every day that you got to play on the MCG.

He was the last to leave the ground at the close of play, walking off alone about a minute after the rest of the team.

After congratulating Jimbo and Cam for their stand, I walked quickly towards the library. I wanted to find out if David had managed to discover any more news about cricketers playing their last Test match here. But when I arrived, the door to the library was locked; the area outside it deserted.

When I got back upstairs, the England players and coaches had all joined our team. I grabbed a bottle of water and immediately made a line towards Freddy, who was sitting on his own.

'Hey, well batted today.' He looked at me. His eyes looked pale and red — as if he'd been crying.

'It's a harsh sun you have out here.' His head moved slowly as he turned to look at me. It was the last thing I'd expected him to say.

'Yeah, well we've been lucky with the cloud cover. Sometimes in February and March it gets over 40 here.'

'Forty?' he looked puzzled. Maybe they used Fahrenheit in England, like they did in America.

'Um, very, very hot.' He leant back and sighed, a slight smile on his face.

'What's your highest score?' I asked. I thought he mustn't have heard me. I was about to repeat the question but Freddy stood up suddenly, glancing about the room as if searching for something.

'Where you heading, Fred?' one of the England coaches asked, his face showing concern. Perhaps they had noticed some odd behaviour. Freddy muttered something incoherent and pushed his way out of the room. I got up and followed.

'Toby?' I almost crashed into Ally, who was standing outside the doorway with Rahul and Jay.

'Hey, guys, did you see which way that kid went?'

'Toby, there's something wrong,' Jay said, grabbing my arm. I shrugged it off.

'Guys, this is important.' I broke away and headed up the ramp, looking right and left.

'Listen, Toby.' There was a sense of urgency in Ally's voice that made me stop. 'Something's happened to Georgie. We can't find her.'

'What do you mean, you can't find her? Have you tried her phone? Didn't she say where she was going?'

'Of course we have,' Ally snapped.

I had to think fast. I was worried that Freddy might do something crazy. I wasn't sure exactly why, but I didn't trust the Grubber and I was the only person who could help him.

'Listen. Go in and grab Jimbo. Get him to get my phone and ring David, the MCC librarian. His number's on my phone.'

'What will *he* do?' Jay asked, looking sceptical.

'More than I can do,' I snapped back. 'He knows this place. He knows the security people.'

'I thought she was your best friend?' Ally said, eyeing me keenly.

'And, Toby, you were the last one to see her. Did she say anything? Where she was going?' Rahul sounded anxious.

'What do you mean I was the last one to see her?' And then I stopped. 'Oh no,' I said, my stomach tightening suddenly. Ally stepped forward.

'What is it, Toby?' She looked worried.

'Go and see David,' I snapped. It came out harsher than I meant it, but my words had the desired effect and they moved off to find David. I turned and ran before any of them could change my mind. I wasn't sure I could do this on my own.

The MCG was an enormous space, and although it was virtually empty, hunting down Freddy would be like looking for a needle in a haystack.

'Freddy!' I shouted, bounding down the escalators in the Members area four steps at a time. A few people turned to look. 'Have you seen a guy, um, a kid wearing cricket gear go past this way?' I asked a group of adults. One of them looked me up and down, frowning.

'Well, ten minutes ago there was a group of them on the oval playing cricket.' The others laughed. I smiled, pretending to find his joke funny. The oval. Maybe that's where Freddy, or should I say the Grubber inside him, would go. Back to the place he knows best: the MCG pitch.

I was on the lower level but still had access to the ground. Sure enough, on the far side of the oval, walking around the perimeter beneath the Southern Stand, was the lone figure of Freddy.

There was no gate at the bottom, so I hurdled the fence and ran onto the ground, then stopped suddenly. Maybe it would be best if I sneaked around the stands so he didn't see me, though what if I couldn't get all the way around?

But it was too late; he'd seen me. He started jogging. I sprinted after him, angling myself across the ground so I'd intercept him — as long as he kept running in the same direction. But he stopped, and darted up into the outer. Veering right so I would avoid the pitch and the groundsmen out there working on it, I ran across the ground, trying to keep track of his movements.

By the time I'd got to the other side, he was out of sight again. I ran through the open gate and turned left, just managing to catch a glimpse of him as he headed towards the stairs at the back of the stand.

Pulling the cricket ball out of my pocket, I slowed momentarily, took aim and hurled it at Freddy. It missed him by millimetres, smacking into the top of the stairs and rebounding back towards me. Grabbing it, I stumbled up the steps after him.

'Freddy!' I panted, looking up. 'You've got to stop!' From somewhere above came a horrible screaming sound. 'Freddy!'

I could hear him still climbing the steps, but his footsteps were getting slower. I threw the ball again as he was climbing the next flight of stairs, this time hitting him on the back leg. He slowed briefly, but then regained his balance, and struggled on.

'The curse,' I hissed, angrily. I'd forgotten to say the four words. I scampered up the next flight of stairs, hoping that Freddy wasn't going all the way to the top deck of the Southern Stand. But as I rounded the corner, I knew straight away that he wasn't.

With a grim smile on his face, Freddy was slowly walking backwards towards the edge of the second level.

'No, Freddy!' I called, frozen to the spot. 'Stop!' But he kept on moving. I could just make out the top of the huge sheet of material with my name splashed all over it. So this is where they had all sat, I thought, then shook my head, surprised that I could be thinking such a thing at a moment like this.

Freddy's face was bright red and his body was heaving up and down, his mouth gulping desperately as he tried to suck air into his lungs.

'You will destroy us both,' he wheezed, continuing to walk backwards towards the edge.

I'm close enough to hit him, I thought, rotating the ball carefully in my hand so that the seam was over my index and big finger. From somewhere to our left a voice cried out. There was another scream. I looked across and almost fell over with shock. I was up on the big screen, along with Freddy. Someone was filming us now. I dropped my hand, suddenly nervous that there were people watching me. I paused, wondering if I'd get as good an opportunity again. In a flash the decision was clear; there would be time for explanations later.

Suddenly my arm was up and the ball was fizzing towards Freddy.

'You've been caught out!' I screamed. The ball made a whooshing noise as it spun through the air before connecting with Freddy's neck. He stumbled back, his fingers frantically reaching for air as he lost his balance and fell onto the edge of the stand.

'No!' I yelled, rushing forward. But it was too late. As if in slow motion, he toppled over. I watched in horror as he plunged over the edge, at the last moment clutching the sheet. There was a great ripping noise as his fingers caught onto the enormous piece of cloth.

I grabbed a hunk of rope and material still attached to the stand. For a split second nothing happened, then suddenly I was jerked forward, my stomach smashing into the concrete wall, forcing the air out of my lungs. I hung onto the thin rope tied to the ledge, praying that it wouldn't give way. Every muscle in my body strained with the exertion of holding him steady. How far was he from the ground below?

There were more screams then the sound of feet and voices.

'Hold on!' I heard someone yell. And then, 'Let go, son. We'll catch you!' But the weight I was fighting against didn't budge. I felt a pair of hands, and then another pair, press in close and slowly I let go.

'The kid's paralysed with fear,' someone shouted.

'Freddy! It's me. You're okay,' one of his team mates called from below. They must have seen what was happening on the scoreboard or on the monitors inside the dressing rooms, and all rushed over.

'Jesus, Freddy, come on!' Freddy's knuckles grasping the torn sheet were white, and his face was frozen in terror. He was in total shock. He was only a few metres above a mass of outstretched arms, waiting to receive him.

I bent down, picked up the ball, and aimed at the small section of sheet just above his hands.

'He's coming down now,' I yelled. 'Hit his hands,' I whispered to the ball, then threw it firmly at his outstretched fingers. The ball hit him directly on the knuckles and he immediately lost his grip. Freddy was caught by eight pairs of arms and gently lowered to the ground.

'He's okay,' I said, as everyone suddenly turned to look at me.

'Everything's under control.' A man in a dark suit with a kind face had suddenly taken over.

'Brian Casboult?' I whispered, looking up into his face.

'A pleasure to meet you, Mr Toby Jones. I have heard so much about you.'

7 What about Jim?

Saturday — evening

'Something very strange is happening and I am at a loss to explain it,' the England coach, Ken Rummins, said to Mr Casboult, the chief executive of the MCG. We were sitting in his office, up in the top level of the Members Grandstand. 'And especially the actions of the young man sitting in the office here with us,' he added, turning to glare at me.

'I understand your concern, Ken,' Mr Casboult nodded. 'Please be assured that what Toby did was in the interest of Freddy.'

'Interest of Freddy?' Ken Rummins scowled. 'Chasing the poor lad halfway around the ground here, throwing cricket balls at him and almost causing his death? I beg your pardon, Brian, but I don't quite follow the logic of your argument.' How much did Brian Casboult know? I wondered. How much was I going to have to explain? If ever I needed Jim's calm and gentle presence, it was now.

The phone in the coach's top pocket buzzed.

'Yes?' he snapped. I stole a glance at Mr Casboult. He smiled, nodding his head. 'I'm with the lad now.' Mr Rummins looked across at me, a puzzled expression on his face. 'No, by all means. Bring him up.' He snapped his phone shut thoughtfully. 'Well, Freddy is much improved and would like to talk with you.'

I nodded, not sure what to say.

'Ken,' Mr Casboult continued. 'A gentleman by the name of Jim Oldfield has — how can I explain — made contact with cricketers from another place.'

'Another time and place,' I added, nodding.

'Yes. Now I am not fully familiar with all the details, but I have called our librarian back, Mr David Howie, and I know he can clarify the situation further.'

'I can explain, Mr Casboult,' I said.

'I think you've done quite enough,' Mr Rummins snapped, standing up suddenly and walking towards the window. 'I presume that what was shown on the scoreboard there has been recorded and will be available?'

'I saved his life,' I blurted out, unable to control my anger any longer. 'Freddy had been taken over by one of the Grubbers. I saw him come onto the field and approach Freddy while I was batting.' The two men were staring at me, but I wasn't going to stop now. 'The longer that Grubber stayed inside him the harder it would have been to get him out.'

'A what?' the coach finally asked.

'A Grubber. It's like a spirit. A spirit of a past Test player wanting to play cricket again.'

'You're talking rubbish, lad.'

'It's all right, Toby. We'll sort this matter out,' Mr Casboult reassured me.

'If it wasn't for the lads down there, I'd cancel this game here and now,' the coach continued. Mr Casboult was saved from replying by a light knock on the door.

'Mr Rummins,' I pleaded, walking towards him. 'Just tell me one thing. Was Freddy's behaviour different when he came off the field today? Does he always bat like that?' Mr Casboult opened the door. 'Well?'

Mr Rummins turned from the window and looked at me. 'I'll be honest with you. No, he wasn't his normal self. Not at all.' He looked down at his feet, his voice quieter. 'He normally bats at six ...'

'He wasn't wearing a helmet,' I hissed, as Mr Casboult ushered Freddy and an England official into the room. We both turned.

'Toby?' Freddy stepped forward shyly, holding out his hand. The manager of the England team stood behind him.

'Now wait on a moment, Freddy,' Mr Rummins began, trying to step in between us. He was keen to keep the atmosphere tense.

'Hi,' I said, shaking his hand. 'Toby Jones. Listen, I'm really sorry about what happened out there.

Um . . .'

'I think we can leave these two boys here to chat for a while, don't you, Ken?' Brian Casboult said, walking towards the door.

'Well, I'm not sure that's a wise thing. What if . . .'

'Come on, Ken,' the England manager said. 'The Aussies are shouting the bar tonight and they've arranged a highlights package of the 2005 Test series.' Ken Rummins hesitated.

'It's okay, Mr Rummins.' Freddy looked up at him. 'In a funny, weird sort of way.'

'Here,' the manager said, taking a business card out of his pocket. 'You ring me at once if there's any problem, you hear?' Mr Casboult rolled his eyes gently and winked at me.

'No throwing English cricketers through glass windows,' he whispered as he walked past me.

'Promise,' I mouthed back.

Freddy and I stayed up in the office for the next half-hour. We found a supply of snacks and a small fridge well stocked with all sorts of drinks.

'Are you sure he won't mind?' he asked, as I threw him a bottle of lemon mineral water.

'I reckon he can afford it,' I laughed. I told Freddy the entire story — from the time I first met Jim and discovered I had the ability to use *Wisden*s to travel back in time. He listened attentively, only once stopping me to ask a question. It was a question others had asked me too.

'Can you take me?'

'Sure I could. But I've got a few other problems I have to solve.' I asked Freddy to explain what it was like having the Grubber in him. Was he conscious of what was happening?

'It was very strange,' he said, after a pause. 'It was like I had moved outside my body and I was watching from a distance. I couldn't work out what was going on. And then slowly I sensed myself drifting back in.'

'In?'

'Into my body. I was saying things and hearing what I was saying but not really wanting to say them. But after a while it got easier. I sort of got more confident. But someone was talking for me; making decisions that I normally wouldn't make.'

'Like wanting to bat second drop?'

'Yes. And then refusing to put the helmet on. That was very strange. When the wicket fell, I went to pick it up, but for some reason I walked straight past it. I can remember one of the guys stopped me. Told me I'd forgotten it.'

'And what did you say?'

'I've never used one before and I'm not going to start using one now.'

'Which, of course, isn't true.'

'No. I've been wearing them ever since I could hold a cricket bat.'

'And what did the coaches say?'

'Well, I was striding out of the room by then, but I think I heard Mr Rummins say, "Give him an over. He'll come to his senses."'

'And then you belted us all round the park and they probably thought let's not change anything here; Freddy's on fire.'

I was enjoying chatting to Freddy but I had to get in contact with Ally and the others and see what was happening with Georgie. 'Freddy, is there anyone else on your team that might have been got at?' I asked, standing.

He shook his head. 'No. Everyone's their normal selves.'

'Okay, well you keep me posted on stuff. Let me know first thing if there's something bothering you.'

'And you'll come with your magic cricket ball.'

'Something like that,' I grinned.

'Can I have a look at it?' he asked. I pulled it out of my pocket. Mr Casboult had got one of the security guys to retrieve it from the seats in the stand.

'It just looks like a normal cricket ball,' he said, turning it around in his hand.

'I know. But believe me, it's not.'

'Yeah, well just don't use it on us tomorrow.'

'If you bat like you did today I might need to.' I caught the ball from him and put it back in my pocket.

'I don't think I'll ever hit the ball like that again,' he sighed, standing up.

'Freddy, remember — that wasn't you hitting the ball.'

'Can you find out who it was?'

'Yeah, well we're working on it.' We shook hands, promising to catch up again either later that evening or some time tomorrow. I couldn't wait to tell Jim what had happened, but first I needed to find Ally and the rest of them and see if they'd heard from Georgie.

8 Inside the Scoreboard

Saturday — evening

'Hey!' I almost ran over Ally as I burst through the door. She and the others had been waiting just outside. 'Any news?' She shook her head.

'We were told not to disturb you,' Rahul said, staring at Freddy as he passed us with a smile and a wave.

'Is he the guy you threw the ball at?' Jay asked. 'What were you thinking?' I explained the situation as briefly and as quickly as possible. A worrying thought had been nagging away at me ever since Ally had first mentioned that Georgie was missing.

'Georgie came out onto the field,' I explained. 'And that's where the Grubber was. Maybe there was another one of them out there?'

'Surely someone would have seen him?' Rahul said.

'No, that's the whole point. I think I'm the only one who can see them. And Jim, of course.'

'That'd be right,' Jay said, sullenly. 'It's always just Toby. You're the time traveller; you're the Cricket Lord; you're the kid who gets to ...'

'Oh, shut up, Jay,' Ally snapped. 'It's the way it is.'

'It's not as if I went looking for this,' I explained. I sensed that Jay had always found it difficult to come to terms with the fact that I'd stumbled upon Jim and the time travel. Perhaps his sudden outburst wasn't that surprising. Ally rested a hand on my forearm.

'What do we do?' she asked, steering me towards the other side of the room.

'Are you sure Georgie's nowhere about?'

'We've searched the entire place.'

'We've been doing nothing else for the entire afternoon,' Jay said, turning from the window.

'Even the security people have been searching,' Rahul added.

'I got around to most of them and showed them the picture I have of her on my phone,' Jay added.

'What about her mum? Does she know?' I asked.

Ally looked down, avoiding eye contact. 'We wanted to wait until we'd told you. We thought maybe there was a special place here.' Her voice trailed.

'I'm going to go and check on Jim. Now that I'm a Cricket Lord it doesn't matter so much if I revisit a place I've been before.'

'Toby, are you sure?' Ally looked horrified, obviously recalling the frightening experiences she'd had seeing herself in the past.

'I'm a Cricket Lord. Jim explained it to me. I can stay for unlimited periods of time and won't be harmed if I meet myself.'

'What good is that going to do?' Jay asked.

I took a deep breath. 'Jim might know where a Grubber could have taken her,' I explained.

'If that's what's happened,' Jay said, looking doubtful. 'She probably just got bored watching the cricket here and went into town to go shopping.'

'So why isn't she answering her phone?'

'I told you — the battery's probably flat. Or she's watching a movie and turned it off.' I looked at Ally. She was shaking her head.

'No way. She would have told me.' She glanced at me. 'How long will you be?'

'Not long. Just long enough to check on Jim and give him an update.'

'Toby, we'll wait here, okay?' Rahul gave me an encouraging pat on the back.

'Are you sure? Aren't you due home soon?'

'Leave it to us,' Rahul smiled.

'Can you tell Jimbo what's happening? He might be wondering where the heck I am. Oh, yeah. I'll need someone to guide my eyes to a zero in the *Wisden*.'

'I'll do that!' Rahul said quickly.

'Yeah, that'd be right. You got to go to India. You . . .' Jay complained.

'Hey!' Rahul threw his hands up. 'It's okay, Jay. You can. It's not like I'm going to time travel again.'

'Come on, Jay. You do it.' Maybe letting Jay help would settle him down a bit and make him a bit more pleasant to be around.

Ally smiled. 'Don't be long, okay?'

I had a moment of panic when I pushed at the locked library door, but then remembered that I had a *Wisden* upstairs in the room Jimbo and I were sharing during the cricket camp.

'Any zero?' Jay asked, opening up the *Wisden*.

'Yep. Just make sure it's from a cricket score and not a nought or something in writing.'

'Hey, I know what to do. Here we go.'

'Yeah, well just put my finger exactly on the spot and then let go, okay?' I looked into the grey swirl of numbers and letters, just managing to make out a round zero next to my finger. 'Okay?' But Jay wasn't letting go.

'Are you sure you've got it?' he asked.

'Jay!' I felt his hand release my finger as the rushing sound whooshed into my head. But as I sensed myself drifting away, he grabbed my hand again.

'Nooooo. Jay?' In slow motion I spun around, desperately trying to shake off his grip, but he held firm and I knew suddenly it was too late. If I did let go of him, who knows where he'd end up? The whooshing sound ebbed away slowly and I was left with that numb, empty feeling of being somewhere, but nowhere.

I pushed Jay off me and got to my feet. I immediately felt the coldness pressing in, and the mist made it hard to see past the clump of trees we'd arrived next to.

'Just shut up, Jay, and do as I say, all right?'

Jay held up his hands in surrender. 'Hey, no worries. You didn't tell me we were coming back here.'

'Jay!' I snapped, glaring at him angrily. 'I ...' And then my voice was sucked away and I was gasping for air.

'Toby?' Jay's voice sounded miles away. My feet lifted off the ground slightly, and suddenly I was flying backwards through the air, my arms outstretched, fingers clawing at nothing but empty space.

'Jaaaaaaaaaaaaaaaaaay!' My voice was lost, drifting into nothingness. I caught a glimpse of Jay's horrified face; he was too shocked to even move. Swinging my arms and legs to try and get balanced, I managed to glance around, just in time to see another Toby, standing alone, a cricket ball in his hand.

'Oh no,' I muttered, closing my eyes. 'TOBY!' I roared, trying to make my other self aware of what was about to happen. I was 10 metres away and closing in fast. Then my body swung upwards, and I spun around slightly, adopting the exact same position and stance as the Toby from only hours before.

Bracing myself, I waited for the two bodies to meet, but instead of a bone-crunching collision I felt nothing but a weird, melting feeling as I stopped, merging into the Toby Jones standing there, arm outstretched, about to throw the ball.

Was I me? Or was I now the Toby of earlier today?

'Jay!' I called, looking back up the hill towards the group of trees near the spot where we'd arrived. If I was me, surely Jay would be there. There was no answer. I set off in the direction I'd come from. There was also no sign of any Grubbers. 'Jay, can you hear me?'

'Toby?' Jay appeared from behind one of the dead-looking trees, shivering.

'Thank God,' I gasped. I ran up to him and then stopped suddenly. His mouth was hanging open. 'What?' I asked.

'Toby?' He took a step backwards, his eyes wide with fright.

'What?' I gasped as I looked down at myself. There was nothing to see! I put my hands in front of my face; I was only just able to discern their outline.

'Oh no,' I moaned, a feeling of dread washing over me. Of course it was too good to be true that nothing would happen. 'Come on, we've got to find Jim.'

'Does that mean we're going over there?' I followed Jay's gaze towards the oval. There didn't appear to be any Grubbers anywhere.

'Come on,' I said, jogging across an open area. We ran for a few minutes, climbing a small rise, and then picked up a track that wound down to the oval on the opposite side of the scoreboard, which loomed over the ground, casting an eerie shadow of darkness on the far side.

'Hey, there he is!' Jay shouted. A solitary figure was slowly making his way up the grassy hill beneath the scoreboard itself.

'Are you sure?' I asked as we both sprinted around the rows of seats.

'Jim?' I called. The figure stopped and turned. Slowly he raised an arm in the air. Relieved, I rushed forward, Jay just behind me.

'What?' I asked, seeing the look of anguish on Jim's face. 'Am I going to be all right?'

'Toby, my dear boy, of course you are,' he said, trying to smile. He was looking past me. I turned around suddenly.

'They're not playing!'

Jim nodded slowly. The two old umpires were standing in the middle of the pitch. Some fielders were slowly making their way towards a small green gate and the batters were standing with the rest of the fielders.

'Are they real?' Jay asked.

'This game is the spirit of cricket. They are real enough, but when a player leaves the field, he disappears forever. He never returns.' Jim turned to me.

'Toby, have you got the ball with you?'

'Jim, what . . .'

'Give me the ball.' I took it from my pocket and passed it to him. 'You won't feel anything, Toby. Just don't catch the ball.' Before I knew what was happening, Jim had thrown it firmly in my direction. I ducked instinctively, raising an arm to my face, but the ball followed me. There was a hissing sound as it connected with my shoulder, then nothing.

'No way!' Jay gasped, staring from me to the ball a few metres behind me.

'That cricket ball, Toby, is your protection as a Cricket Lord.'

'I ran into myself,' I said. I bent down to retrieve the ball and noticed that I could now see my arm again. I looked down to check that my body and legs were also clearly visible.

'Yes, and because you are now a Cricket Lord, there were also no unfortunate consequences.'

'But what about when I was here before? How come I didn't sense or see the later me?'

Jim sighed. 'Because you are different, Toby,' he said, finally.

'You mean different as in three hours older?'

'No, I mean different. You have taken on powers that your former self could not have seen. But listen, you need to return.' He glanced up at the enormous scoreboard.

'What's going to happen?' I asked.

The umpires were now walking towards the far set of stumps. From high above us came a creaking, groaning sound. Another '0' was being put up on the scoreboard.

'As long as I am here all will be well,' Jim said.

'But you can't stay here forever, Jim.' I couldn't imagine leaving him in this cold, desolate place.

'For the good of cricket, Toby, I can stay here forever.'

'C'mon, Toby,' Jay muttered, pulling on my sleeve. 'You heard him. Let's get out of here.'

'Jim, will Father Time stay up there?' I braved another glance up at the scoreboard, wondering about the being working the numbers inside it. Was he a man? Could he see us now?

'Father Time has been stripped of all his powers. But now that the game is stopping he's becoming a threat again. It was once thought that one of the Grubbers here was his younger sibling, who unlike the rest of the Grubbers remained loyal to him. But years and years have passed and nothing has changed.'

'Until now.' I turned again to look out over the ground. No one appeared to have moved since I last looked.

'You must leave now!' Jim ordered.

'I know,' I muttered. There was not a Grubber in sight. The stands around the ground were empty. Dark clouds rushed across the sky and I could feel drops of rain. Beside me, Jay was shivering.

'Toby, take this and return to the MCC library.'

Jim had taken the scorecard from his pocket. Jay whistled softly. It was the ticket that enabled anyone to travel back in time. All they had to do was place it inside a *Wisden*; any *Wisden*. 'Find David and ask him for the first edition of *Wisden*. Toby, are you listening?'

'Yes, of course,' I said. I refused to believe that this was the end, yet there was something very final in Jim's voice.

'Father Time requires only three things to restore himself to the way he used to be. Two of these items we can destroy now.'

'The first *Wisden* and the scorecard?' I asked.

'Yes. Placing the scorecard anywhere inside the first *Wisden* restores time for the person holding the card. Of course, if the scorecard is destroyed, so too is any chance that it might save us from Father Time.'

I was finding it hard to follow Jim. 'What's the other thing?'

Jim looked at me, as if weighing up whether he wanted to tell me. Finally he spoke. 'A Cricket Lord. This is why it is imperative that you return and remove yourself from his clutches.'

'But you're a Cricket Lord too. If you come back as well then he'll never get all three things.'

'He needs to be stopped, Toby. He will come after you, or me, and he will not give up. Ever.'

'HELP!' a voice called to our left. We all froze. 'TOBY!'

'That's Georgie,' I cried, sprinting towards the scoreboard.

'Toby,' Jim called. 'Wait!' I slowed as he and Jay caught up to me.

'That was Georgie. I'm sure of it,' I said, my heart pounding.

'She's been missing most of the day,' Jay added.

'And she came onto the oval,' I added.

'Georgie walked onto the oval?' Jim gasped. He looked anxiously up at the scoreboard.

'What's happened to her?'

Jim glanced at me quickly.

'A Grubber, but she is fighting. She must have seen you.' I scanned the board but could see nothing. There were three square holes but nothing moved behind them.

'I'm going up,' I said. 'We can't just leave her there.'

'Jay, go back to the ground. Wait over there by the gate. You must keep the game going. As long as there is one person watching, the game must go on.'

'But hang on. You can't leave me out here ...' he protested.

'Jay,' Jim said, firmly. 'Do as I say.' Jay muttered something under his breath and stalked off to the other side of the ground.

9 Into the Scoreboard

Saturday — evening

'Stay behind me and don't speak,' Jim said, as we marched up the incline towards a metal ladder.

'I'll follow ...'

'Toby, do not enter the scoreboard. That is an order.'

I waited at the bottom watching Jim slowly and carefully make his way up the rusty metal rungs. He paused at the top, took something from his pocket and held it up to the door. There was a click and a small trap door swung open wide. A cloud of white dust billowed from the entrance.

Jim turned once, waved, then quickly disappeared into the scoreboard. I turned at the sound of clapping on the field. The players and umpires appeared to be taking up their positions again.

I waited for a few minutes. No sound came from inside the score box. Taking a last look around, I put one foot on the first step of the ladder.

From above came a sudden crashing sound. It sounded like something heavy falling.

'Jim, are you okay?' I called up, then spun around, startled by a noise to my right. Two Grubbers were swooping in towards me. Perhaps they had heard the commotion as well. I took a few paces back but they didn't appear to notice me, as they approached the stairs. What was happening in there? Was Jim in trouble? They flew up the steps, barely touching the rungs, and disappeared into the gloom. I waited a few seconds then followed them.

The interior of the scoreboard was dark and smelt old and stale. There must have been at least three levels.

'Jim?' I whispered. I could hear nothing but the faint sound of footsteps moving away from the entrance. Behind me it looked like play was about to resume. Was that because of the three of us being here?

I was in a dark, dusty chamber. Huge black wooden boards were lying about the place, some covered in white names. The air was thick with chalk dust. I crept slowly along the left edge, a shaft of light from the only opening guiding me to the opposite side of the chamber and another ladder, smaller than the first, attached to the side wall.

Again I paused, listening for the slightest sound. I could hear shuffling footsteps on the floor above, or perhaps even two levels up. I stepped onto the ladder. Someone was talking.

'Jim?' I called softly, taking another few steps up the ladder. Something or someone crashed against a wall. The whole scoreboard shook. Shocked, one of my hands slipped and I swung out on the ladder, crashing against the side wall. Regaining my balance, I swung back and clambered up the final steps.

The room I stood in was almost empty, like the one below. This level was lighter, with more openings out onto the ground. On one side of the room was an old chair and table. A massive scorebook lay open on the table, covering most of its top. Littered about the room were black wooden squares, numbered on both sides. There were lots of 1s covering the wall to my right; which meant that zeroes were visible on the other side.

'Get out!' a voice screamed from the level above. Jim? Was he talking to me? I ran across the room and climbed the final flight of stairs.

'Georgie!' I yelled. Georgie stood with her back to the wall; her face was white, and her eyes were bulging. Beyond her, two Grubbers were dragging Jim towards a long, rectangular opening. There was no sign of anyone else. Maybe Father Time wasn't here. Jim had been lifted off his feet and was being moved towards the opening.

'No!' I yelled, grabbing my cricket ball and hurling it as hard as I could at the nearest Grubber. I remembered the words. A stench filled the air suddenly as the Grubber stumbled and fell, but the other had a tight hold on Jim and was shoving him through the opening.

'Let go!' I screamed, rushing forward to pick up the ball. The first Grubber was still lying on the ground, his body twisted and curled in pain. I took hold of Jim's shoulder, desperately trying to pull him back.

'Georgie! Please help!' I yelled, glancing at her briefly. She hadn't moved. It looked as if she hadn't heard me. Feeling my hold on Jim slipping, I lobbed the ball weakly at the other Grubber, muttering the words as it caught him on the shoulder.

Jim's head and shoulders were protruding through the gap. His body jerked and slid further forward as the Grubber opposite me briefly released him. The stench of burning was overbearing.

'Hang on, Jim,' I breathed, slowly hauling him back into the chamber. We collapsed onto the dusty floor. But as I reached out to pick up the ball, I felt a cold hand press down hard on my arm. The second Grubber leant over me, a sickly grin on his face. A thin trail of brown smoke drifted into the air from where the ball had caught him, but the force of my throw hadn't been strong enough.

His face moved in closer and I knew that if I didn't do something quickly I would be overcome like Georgie and Freddy had been. Reaching out, my fingers stretched taut, I got a fingernail onto the seam of the ball, just managing to roll it backwards.

As the Grubber pressed his face into mine, I rammed the ball in front of his nose, pushing it upwards. There was a loud grinding noise and a stream of putrid liquid steamed over me as he screamed, jerking and writhing in agony. I could hear his raspy breath and feel the jagged, pointy bones of his rib cage pressing into me. He was somewhere between spirit and body; his flesh was rotten and stinking. He was older than any living thing should be, somehow being kept alive by the mean spirit that dwelled inside him.

His face was just centimetres from mine and I watched in horror as his old, wrinkled skin suddenly shrank, twisting and screwing his face into a pinched scowl. His hair was changing colour from grey to white and falling out in clumps. A tooth fell from somewhere, then another one. I squeezed my eyes shut so I didn't have to look into his gummy, foul-smelling mouth.

Kicking out with as much force as I could, I rolled away from beneath the Grubber, struggling hard not to vomit.

'Get out of here,' Jim called harshly.

'Is Georgie okay?'

'Who?' Jim lay slumped against the side wall, his head resting on his shoulder. There was still no sign of Father Time. Perhaps the fight had taken its toll. 'Jim, where's Father Time?' Jim looked up slowly. 'Jim, are you all right?' He nodded absently.

'Father Time,' he said, finally. 'He has been dealt with. Go now.'

'Were they Grubbers?' The two beings lay shrivelled and curled on the dusty wooden floor. I'd thought Grubbers were spirits. How had they been able to man-handle Jim? Maybe there were different types of Grubbers — spirits that could possess people and ones with a physical form.

'They are bodily guards. They were called to guard Father Time. He obviously recruited some of the Grubbers and was able to maintain their physical form in some way. But go now, before they build up their strength again.'

'But what about you, Jim? Won't they try and attack you again?'

'Toby, when you have gone I will deal with them. But not in front of your eyes.'

'Do I still have to destroy the scorecard and the first *Wisden*?' I wasn't sure that Jim had heard me. Still holding the ball, I turned to face Georgie. She was rooted to the spot, staring absently at the scene in front of her. 'It's okay, Georgie,' I said, drawing my arm back. 'This doesn't hurt at all.'

Closing my eyes, I shouted, 'You've been caught out'; then threw the ball firmly at Georgie's left leg. She buckled over, her face momentarily twisted in agony, then slowly slumped to the floor. 'Georgie?' I said, rushing over to her and helping her sit up. 'Speak to me?' I turned her head towards me, searching her eyes for some sign of recognition, but she stared back at me blankly.

'Jim, it didn't work!' I screamed, turning on him. Jim raised a wavering arm and pointed at the square boards.

'Score,' he gasped, then closed his eyes. 'Quickly.' His voice was raspy and faint. I understood straight away what he meant. Hurling myself down the ladder, I got to the middle level then rushed over to a window. The umpire was signalling something, his arm outstretched.

'No ball,' I muttered, desperately searching for the extras sign. Sticking my head outside one of the open windows, I glanced back at the front of the board. I finally found it beneath the total score.

'Here!' I called out, drawing aside a small wooden peg. I pulled back the wooden number displayed. It was a 4. I flipped it over and slammed the board back into its spot, pushing it flat, then pushed the peg back to keep it in place.

'Well done,' Jim said, slowly making his way down the stairs.

'What about Georgie?'

Jim lifted his head. 'Go and collect the first *Wisden* and the scorecard, Toby. Hide it away somewhere that only you know about. I can help Georgie; she's safe here with me.'

'But you said they had to be destroyed.' For a moment Jim looked at me blankly. His right eye was twitching. I'd never seen that happen before.

'Please!' he whispered. His face was grey and streaked with sweat and his eyes looked distant; empty. I leant forward closer, trying to catch the words he was saying.

'In ... scorecard ... first *Wisden*. Save you ... first *Wisden* ...'

Then suddenly his head lolled back and he fell to the floor. For ten minutes I cradled his head in my lap, whispering his name, tears streaming down my face. Slowly his breathing became more regular as his body relaxed.

I tried to make him comfortable but the movement stirred him.

'Jim, what happened? Are you okay?' I scanned his face, desperately hoping for a smile that would make everything all right again.

'Toby.' His voice was dry and hoarse. Slowly he got to his feet. 'Go now.'

'Why?'

'Go!' he roared, turning on me. I flinched, taking a step backwards. He took a deep breath. 'Toby, I am sorry. Please, just do as I say.' Perhaps the short battle with Father Time had affected Jim in some way.

'How *did* you defeat him?' I couldn't believe that it had all happened so quickly. We both glanced through a long window, hearing the sound of ball hitting bat.

'It is done. I will look after the scoring here and Georgie too.'

'You were *stronger* than Father Time?' I persisted, wanting to find out what had happened. Jim took out a zero and replaced it with a two.

'He was much weakened because of his time in this wretched place,' Jim said, pushing home the number. He walked to the table where the large scorebook was and made an adjustment.

'David won't like me borrowing the first *Wisden*. You know how much he treasures that copy.'

'Who?' Jim was looking out through one of the windows at the game below.

'David, the librarian. You know.' Jim had become very vague.

'Well, you're going to have to do what you have to do. Your friend Georgie needs that *Wisden*, Toby.'

'Will the Grubbers return to the game now?'

'I believe they will. The ones you have hit with your cricket ball will at least ensure that the Timeless Cricket Match will continue in the short term.' There was a shout from the field. 'More runs, Toby. Off you go.'

I took a last glance at Jim and moved quickly to the stairs.

Jay hadn't moved from his spot in front of the small stand on the far side of the ground. I noticed a few Grubbers watching from the hill further on.

'Geez, you took your time,' he snapped, jumping up.

'Yeah, well I just happened to save Jim from being shoved out of the top floor of the scoreboard,' I muttered, grabbing him by the arm. I spoke the two lines and suddenly the numbing cold was lifted as we vanished from the Timeless Cricket Match.

10 Eavesdropping

Saturday — evening

I left Jay down in the library to explain to Ally and Rahul about Georgie while I went off to grab something to eat and find Jimbo. Ally would have to do some fast talking to explain Georgie's absence to her mum.

'Welcome back to the land of the living,' Jimbo said, patting me on the back when I returned to the corporate box he and I were sleeping in during the cricket camp. Tonight would be our last night.

'You don't know how true that comment is.'

'You've been to the Timeless Cricket Match?'

'Yup.' I told him about the scoreboard and Jim defeating Father Time.

'Just like that?' he asked, surprised.

'Well, yeah. I guess I was a bit amazed at how quickly it happened too. Jim said that Father Time wasn't his former self. He'd been up in that dusty scoreboard for years and years and had lost his strength.'

'I didn't think ghosts and immortals could lose their strength,' Jimbo said, closing his cricket magazine and walking over to the small fridge to grab a drink. I looked up sharply.

'What do you mean, immortals? What do you know about Father Time?'

Jimbo unscrewed the top of his drink bottle and took a swig. 'David rocked up about half an hour ago. He'd got a call from Ally.'

'Oh, is he still here now?' I asked, pulling out my phone.

'Yeah, he will be. He said he was going to wait for them or you to return. Anyway, I think Jim's told him quite a bit about Father Time and stuff.'

'Like?'

'Well, David didn't tell me much. He just said that ...' Jimbo paused, then looked at me nervously. He'd said too much.

'What, Jimbo? You can tell me.'

'Yeah, well he said that there may come a time when Jim doesn't return. Or that if he does, it won't be as Jim.'

'What does that mean?' I said. There was so much happening that I wasn't understanding. Everyone seemed to be speaking in riddles.

'I dunno. That's what I asked David.'

'And what did he say?'

'That he didn't know either.' I sat down on the bed and sighed. Closing my eyes, I lay back on the bed, enjoying the quietness and calm. I felt the cricket ball nestled against my side.

'Hey, they're picking the World Cup team at the moment,' Jimbo said. I sat bolt upright.

'Now?' The World Cup was on in nine days' time, and the Australian team was going to be selected from the squad playing in this match.

'Yup.' Jimbo looked at his watch. 'Want to listen?'

'What do you mean?'

Jimbo smiled. 'David knows where the meeting's happening. Come on.'

'So?' I asked, following Jimbo out into the corridor. 'They're hardly going to say, "Oh, look, it's Toby and Jimbo. Come in, guys. We're just selecting the Under 15 Australian World Cup team and thought you'd like to help us."' Jimbo said nothing. 'Well, can you at least tell me where we're going?'

'Oh, hello, boys,' David called from the bottom of the escalators. 'I was just coming up to look for you.'

'We're just going to ...' Jimbo whispered, winking at David.

'Going to?' David cocked his head to one side.

'You know,' Jimbo hissed. 'What you said before?' David looked at him blankly. 'David! The meeting! Remember?'

'Oh!' David cried, clapping his hands together. 'Yes, well there's really no time for that. I didn't mean that you *would* actually listen.'

I shrugged at David. 'Did you see the others?' I asked him. 'Ally and the two boys?'

'Oh yes. They were very relieved to hear that Georgie is in safe hands with Jim, though I rather think they would have preferred it if she was back here. But Jim must have his reasons.' David frowned, as if he'd forgotten what he was saying. 'Anyway, I'll be back in a minute. Don't leave before I get back,' he called, heading for the café.

'Just a quick listen,' Jimbo said. I shrugged and followed him into David's office.

'Through here,' Jimbo whispered, putting a finger to his lips. He opened a door behind David's study and walked into what looked like a storeroom. He bent down and crawled behind a couch. A shaft of light shone through from the bottom section of wall behind it. I squeezed in next to him and gasped.

Through some sort of vent I could see down into a large meeting room. Six men were gathered around an enormous table, which was littered with folders, papers and an assortment of drinks and snacks. Another guy, who I didn't recognise, stood next to a whiteboard which was covered with names written in various colours.

'We can't be here,' I breathed, but wishing I had some binoculars to see more clearly the names on the whiteboard.

'Okay, go then,' Jimbo said.

I thought I'd stay for a few minutes, just to see if we could actually hear anything. Everyone seemed to be writing except the man out the front. It was as if they'd all been asked to write an answer. Suddenly the guy standing in the front started to speak.

'So, who have you got?' he asked. A familiar voice spoke. His back was to us but I knew it was Marty.

'I've put down Toby Jones.' Jimbo nudged me. I held my breath. 'The kid's got a cricket brain, there's no doubt about it. He's not volatile and when we need someone with a sense of calm, I think he's the guy who's going to deliver.'

'You call his behaviour today calm?' I didn't recognise that voice.

'That was a situation that was out of his control. None of us knows what's going on there. We're here to talk about his cricket ability and nothing else.'

Feeling uncomfortable, I edged back and returned to David's office. He was bent over by a filing cabinet, searching for something.

'Ah, Toby,' he said, looking up. 'Actually, I was just coming to get you. We thought you'd be interested in getting a look at the selection room.'

'We?'

'Jim and I. He was keen for you to maintain your interest in your current cricket games.'

Jimbo joined us. 'One of 'em reckons I'll play Test cricket for Australia one day,' he beamed, collapsing in a chair by the window. 'But yeah, it actually felt a bit dodgy lying there listening.'

'Especially when our names were being mentioned.' I turned back to David. 'But of course I'm interested in my cricket. We're playing a Test match against the Poms and the team for the World Cup is about to be announced.'

'Exactly, Toby.' David nodded, then took a sip of his coffee.

'Well?'

'There are other matters at hand too,' he said, glancing at the door. Jimbo moved over and closed it gently.

'You mean the Grubbers and Father Time?' said Jimbo. 'But Jim's fixed all that. We just have to get Georgie back.'

'And Jim,' I added. 'It's not quite all over. I'm not going to leave him in that grotty scoreboard for the rest of his days —'

'Toby, listen to me.' David's normally light and pleasant voice suddenly sounded serious. 'Jim said two things to me before he left here. The first he was quite emphatic about. On no account are you to return to attempt to rescue him and bring him back.'

'But why?' asked Jimbo.

'Because if Jim leaves that scoreboard the game of cricket will die.' I shook my head angrily. David continued. 'Don't ask me to explain how, Toby. But Jim was adamant. Cricket is dearer to him than anything else.'

'What about his family? How can a game be more important than your family?' I looked into David's eyes, searching for an answer. He didn't have one and he knew it. I didn't know of any family that Jim had, but he was becoming more and more a part of ours.

99

'I don't know, Toby. Really I don't.' I stared out his office window at the lights beyond the Yarra River. For a moment no one spoke, each of us lost in our own thoughts.

'And the second thing?' Jimbo asked, finally.

'Oh yes,' David replied, placing his coffee cup gently on the table. 'He said when things look like they're fixed, that's the time to question and doubt with all your heart, strength and soul. He said you'd both understand, especially you, Jimbo, being a batsman.'

'Yeah, I know what he means,' Jimbo said.

'So do I,' I said. David looked at me, eyebrows raised. I continued. 'Just when you think you're settled in, you've put away a few boundaries, you're seeing the ball well, then bang! You're out.' I clapped my hands on saying the word 'bang', which caused David to jump slightly. 'Sorry,' I muttered.

'No, no, that's quite all right.'

'David,' I said, trying to sound relaxed. 'There's just one other thing. Jim needs a copy of the first *Wisden*.' David spun around, a look of horror on his face.

'1864? I don't think so, Toby.' He couldn't hide a puzzled frown.

'But it's for Georgie.'

'Georgie?'

'I don't exactly know why or how, but Jim said he needs it to help her. It's something about fixing up time problems for people who've been affected by

Father Time. We were going to have to burn it if Father Time was still around.'

David spluttered. 'Burn it? The first ever *Wisden*? Over my dead body.'

'Can I at least see it?' I asked, walking across the library to the *Wisden* section. I scanned the books, working my way back to the very earliest editions. 'Did you say 1864?' I asked, peering closely at the spines. I heard David chuckle softly behind me. 'It's gone!'

'Jim's instructions,' David said.

'But —'

'He said you might come looking for it.'

'Jim did? I don't get it.'

'Toby, nor do I, and I'm his closest friend, outside your family. I'm off to lock up. Don't forget the cricket match you're playing in.'

'Weird,' I muttered, staring out at the lights around the ground as I followed Jimbo up the escalator. 'Why does Jim ask me to get the *Wisden* if he's already hidden it?'

'Do you reckon David knows where it is?' Jimbo asked.

'I dunno. It wouldn't surprise me.' Jimbo stopped at the top of the escalators and turned to me.

'Listen, mate. We've got a monster day of cricket out there tomorrow. How we go might have a big bearing on whether we get selected in the World Cup squad. They'll probably only pick two Victorians.'

'No way! If there are five of us good enough, then five of us should get in. That's how it is with the

Australian Test team. Sometimes there's no one from a particular state. Name the last South Australian to play in the one-day Australian team.' Jimbo shrugged and started walking again.

'You know what I mean, Toby,' he said, softly. And I did. It was time to shelve Grubbers, scoreboards, Jim and Georgie and focus on the game tomorrow. For a night and a day, they would all have to look after themselves.

But if I'd known what was really happening out there in the mists and fogs swirling around the Timeless Cricket Match, the Test against England would have been the last thing on my mind.

11 Back to the Game

Sunday — morning

Cam and Jimbo, our opening pair, continued their steady partnership the following morning. After an hour's play, they had advanced the score to 0–75. The England attack was steady and persistent but unable to make the breakthrough.

'Of course, you realise England hold the Ashes unless we can force the outright,' Marty said, sitting down next to me.

'So, we send out a message with drinks to tell them to get on with it,' Scott said from behind us.

'You think so?' Marty turned around.

'Of course! What's the point of batting out the day? We might as well go down fighting.'

'Sean? Toby? Anyone else? It's drinks next over. We can get a message out then.'

'I agree with Scott,' I said, probably for the first time ever. 'England is slowing it all down. What they don't want is for us to push the pace; force the issue.

There are no over limits or anything, are there, Marty?' He shook his head. 'We pull out stumps at six o'clock, regardless.'

'So, that means there's another five hours of play.' I was thinking aloud. 'We add on, say, another 80 runs before lunch and we've got a lead of about 140. Bat for another hour after lunch and push it out to 210 runs. That gives England three hours to make the runs. Would they go for it?'

'Would we want them to?' Marty asked.

'Yeah, of course,' I said. 'Like Scott says, we go down on the first innings or we go down outright. Either way, we go down. But surely we have to fight for a victory ourselves.' I noticed Scott nodding.

'What do you think, skipper?' We all turned to look at Sean.

'Yeah, it's your call, mate,' Greg said.

'Geez, I dunno,' Sean said finally. 'Isn't this a good chance for us to get some really good batting practice? Out on the MCG. Class bowling attack. I reckon we're no chance for an outright. Once we start forcing the pace, we'll just collapse again.'

I was surprised that Sean was talking so negatively. Maybe, as captain, he wasn't too rapt about the prospect of going down by an innings.

'Well, as Greg says, it's your call, Sean.' Sean looked around.

'Who reckons we should force the pace? Go for it?' Six arms shot up in the air straight away. 'Yeah, well I guess the team has spoken,' he grinned. 'Toby,

go out with the drinks. Scott, go put the pads on.'
Scott was out of his seat in a flash.

'You got it!' Scott cried. In spite of him, I smiled.
Scott saw me smile and stopped at the door. 'Hey —
and, Jones?'

'What?'

'No bloody warm-ups with you bowling!' he
grinned, and raced out.

I grabbed a couple of towels and a few drink
bottles and joined our twelfth man, Kyle van de Brun,
as he walked out onto the ground.

'We're going for it,' I said to Cam and Jimbo.

'Yeah?' Jimbo took a long swig of his drink. 'Sean
said for us to go nice and steady and wear down the
bowlers.'

Cam nodded. 'Well, Sean has seen the light. You
guys are batting beautifully. You're settled and ready
to go.'

The field spread quickly to all parts of the ground
as Cam and Jimbo upped the tempo. Off one over
they hit seventeen runs, including three cracking 4s
in a row by Jimbo off their off-spinner. In the next
over he planted a short ball way over square leg for
six. Surely he'd done enough to get himself selected
for the World Cup squad, I thought, applauding
loudly. He tried to glide the next ball through a
vacant slips area, but only managed to feather a faint
edge through to the keeper.

I looked up at the scoreboard. Ninety-one runs for
Jimbo. None of us were aware he'd got so close to his

century. I recalled the comment he made about playing for Australia and suddenly realised, with absolute confidence and clarity, that he actually would play for Australia. He was the best batter on the two teams by far, not counting Freddy's brief effort. But that wasn't Freddy; that had been a real Test cricketer.

'Just when I was settled,' he grinned at me. I shook his hand, as did everyone else in the dressing room.

Cam followed soon after, and the applause he got from the sparse crowd sprinkled around the stands was just as heartfelt and enthusiastic.

By lunch we had moved to 3–161 with Scott looking ominous. The England guys weren't as chatty during the lunch break, keeping to themselves, but I made a point of seeking out Freddy.

'You guys are batting well,' he said, grabbing another salad roll from the table.

'You won't want to be eating too many of those,' I told him, smiling. 'You guys will be chasing some serious leather this afternoon.'

'You'll be chasing plenty of leather yourself as we run down the target and get the outright,' he replied, quick as a flash. He gave me a gentle whack on the shoulder.

We lost a steady stream of wickets after lunch. I could only manage five runs myself before being caught off the gloves down the leg side. For a moment I thought the umpire was going to give me the benefit of the doubt. I had taken a step towards the dressing room, then froze suddenly. But I think the umpire took my step as a sign that I'd hit it. Slowly he raised his finger.

On the long walk back, I thought of Adam Gilchrist, and how he said that he would always walk if he knew he was out, rather than wait for the umpire to actually give him out. It sounded great, but boy, it was hard. When you were out in the middle, with a few runs, or even a lot of runs next to your name, I realised it took a lot of strength and honesty to turn away and give yourself out, even though the umpire might not have raised his finger.

We declared the innings closed at 8–188. Our last few batters were probably not going to give us many extra runs, but by being in, they would instead be soaking up valuable time — time that we needed to try and get 10 wickets.

We gathered in a close circle halfway between the fence and the pitch, as the England openers walked out to bat. Sean suddenly appeared lost for words.

'Ten wickets,' I said. Scott nodded, flicking the shiny new ball from hand to hand.

'Total commitment in the field,' he yelled, looking around at us. 'Back each other up, right?'

'Attacking fields, Sean,' I said. 'Don't let the runs they score bother you. They don't matter. They win on first innings, they win on the outright. Who cares?'

We broke up and jogged to our positions.

I glanced at the scoreboard from my place at mid-on. England needed 176 runs and they had 75 minutes in this session and a full two-hour session after tea to do it in. 195 minutes. It was nearly a run a minute, but it was definitely possible. I quickly realised why the rules had changed in cricket — it used to be that play would always end at six o'clock, regardless of the number of overs bowled.

We could just play as slowly as possible, grinding out the overs; changing the field, the occasional fake injury. The umpires would probably get annoyed and try and speed things up. Then again, if we were chasing the win, maybe we'd need as many deliveries as possible to get the 10 wickets.

I was a bit disappointed not to be given the new ball, especially as Greg was off the field and not likely to bowl for the rest of the day, but Scott's aggression was a positive and Jaimi, while not super quick, had good accuracy and a mean faster ball.

The runs flowed steadily as England took advantage of the many gaps. Sean had set an attacking field with three fielders in slips, as well as a gully and point. We had no third man or mid-off and the clear, dry air meant the ball wasn't swinging much.

'Bang it in,' I said, jogging over to Jaimi as he prepared to start his third over. 'Get them on the back foot.'

'Pitch is dead,' he replied. I rubbed the ball hard on my trousers, trying to get as much shine as I could

108

on one side of the ball. I could win this game for us, I thought suddenly, thinking of the magic cricket ball, tucked away at the bottom of my bag. But that could never happen. Not even Scott had suggested it.

They knocked another seven runs off Jaimi's over, taking their score on to 0–34. At this rate they would get the runs in about 25 overs. Suddenly the target of 176 was looking much smaller. It was now down to 142. Worse, England still had 10 wickets in hand.

I watched Sean at first slip. He hadn't once spoken to his bowlers or even made a change in the field. Perhaps Wesley had told him not to bother making any changes. Occasionally he clapped his hands in encouragement, but even that had been half-hearted.

'Scott, we've got to try something different,' I said, meeting him at mid-pitch.

'Tell me about it. I wanted to do a bit of leg theory, especially on the left-hander, but Sean says I've got to attack off-stump.'

'Leave it with me,' I said, jogging quickly down to the slips.

'Sean, we need something different. I'm going to field at square,' I said, pointing past the square leg umpire, who was already in position. Sean shrugged. 'Sean, what's the matter?'

'Hey, Toby,' said Wesley. 'Don't hassle him. He's —'

'What are you talking about, Wesley? This is a bloody Test match, not beach cricket. We've got to do something. Now!' I hissed.

'Guys,' Sean said, then suddenly collapsed to the ground. One minute he was standing there, the next he was lying on the turf, moaning softly. I waved frantically towards the dressing room, trying to ignore the twisting knot of fear in my stomach. Was this somehow related to the Grubbers?

'Bloody hell, Jones. What did you do, whack him one?'

'As if, Scott.'

'Okay, you're captain now,' he pressed on, trying to drag me to one side.

'Scott, hang on!' I watched Marty and two other coaches talking softly with Sean, getting down close to his head, and patting him on the back.

'Move back, boys,' a man said, jogging in to join the huddle around Sean. I guessed he must have been a doctor by the way he was dressed. Perhaps he'd been sitting somewhere in the crowd watching the game.

'Do you reckon that's his dad?' someone else said. After a few minutes, Sean was helped to his feet. Supported by the doctor guy and one of the coaches, they made their way slowly from the field.

'Marty?' I called. He jogged over to us.

'Possibly a migraine, but we're not sure. I doubt he'll be back on. Toby, you take over as captain. I'll try and organise one of the England players to sub.'

'Hey, we don't need one of their players,' Scott said, scowling.

'We need all the players we can get,' Wesley said.

'We've lost our fastest bowler, our captain and second spinner and —'

'Yeah, yeah,' Scott growled, glaring at Wesley. 'Put a sock in it. Come on, Toby. What's the plan?' He turned expectantly towards me.

'Okay, Jaimi, fine leg. Jimbo, go to regular mid-wicket. No one else on the leg side. I want —'

'I thought you said we were going short. Attack the body.'

'We are, Scott.'

'But I need some protection. I need more than two bloody fielders out there.'

'Scott, short and fast, yes. But make him hit you from outside off stump. Make the ball come on at him hard. Make the batter think that anything he hits to leg is easy runs.'

'It *is* easy runs,' Wesley muttered.

'Hey, have you got a better idea?' Scott snapped.

'Jaimi, I'll bowl from your end, then bring you back on after Scott's spell, okay?'

'No worries, Toby,' he replied.

Scott charged in and let rip the fastest delivery of the Test match with his first ball after the break. It fizzed past the left-hander's head. Wesley jumped high, but wasn't able to stop it cleanly. He fell to the ground, crying out in pain, as he hurled one of his gloves away.

'Now look what you've done,' he yelled, staring in horror at the blood already congealing inside his inners. Wesley didn't wait for the trainers, but picked up his glove and made for the dressing rooms.

'Hey, we need your equipment!' Scott yelled after him.

'Get your own,' he fired back, not even turning around. We gathered in again, each of us staring despondently in the direction of the dressing rooms, hoping for a miracle. Or at least a wicketkeeper.

'Anyone done any keeping before?' I asked.

'I've done —'

'NO!' we all yelled, turning on Scott.

'Jimbo?'

'I could have a go at it, I guess,' he said, reluctantly.

'Bloody hell, what's *she* doing,' Barton Rivers, our spinner, said. We all turned. I had never been so glad in my life to see Ally, jogging happily towards us, a huge grin on her face. She was fixing her hair as she ran.

'Hey, she's cute,' Callum, our number four batsman, noted. I couldn't help feeling a sense of pride as she joined our group.

'Hey, guys,' she said. 'Where do you want me?'

'Y-you're a girl,' Barton said.

'Shut up, Barton,' Scott said. 'She plays cricket.'

'Ally, you're keeping. You're going to have to go back to the dressing rooms and find whatever gear you need.'

'Got it!' she said, sprinting off.

'What do you mean she's keeping? She's a girl!' Barton said.

'You've already told us that,' Jimbo said, turning towards the dressing rooms. 'Toby, I'll go help her

112

find some gear. I reckon Marty and the rest will be pretty busy with Sean and Wesley.'

The game finally got going again, though without Jimbo, who for some reason was still in the dressing rooms. I could barely recognise the team I'd played with yesterday. There was no Sean, Jimbo, Greg or Wesley. Rahul was out at mid-off, wearing a pair of white shorts and a white, buttoned school shirt. I'd never seen him look so happy. The England team had given us two of theirs, but without Jimbo we were still a player down. Scott finished the rest of his over with a series of short, fast deliveries.

'Just like Riverwall,' Ally called, clapping her gloves together, after she'd made it back onto the field.

I took the ball and started to measure out my run-up. 'Heads up, everyone!'

Rahul looked in my direction. 'I'm playing for Australia, Toby,' he grinned, excitedly. He didn't seem to care about what he was wearing.

The opener played and missed two of my first three balls. I pushed the fourth ball through quicker and fuller. He jabbed his bat down too late, the ball hitting him on the foot instead. I leapt in the air, appealing loudly, turning my back on the batter as he crumpled to the pitch. The umpire didn't hesitate, raising his arm quickly.

We had them rattled. Scott and I bowled without a break until tea, focusing on forcing them back and getting the batsmen in two minds. It worked a treat. Scott had their first drop caught top-edging a mistimed pull, and I snared two more wickets; one with a change of pace, and the other with a nice outswinger. Ally took the catch comfortably in front of her face. They weren't enjoying our aggressive approach and the sudden pace we were generating.

First slip had suddenly become the premium position on the field, but as captain I wasn't letting anyone else take it.

'What happened to Jimbo?' I asked Ally as we walked off for tea.

'Yeah, I dunno,' she replied. 'I was wondering why he didn't show up again. He went looking for a pair of inners for me, but he never returned. I had the choice of either wearing Wesley's blood or going without.'

'Which did you choose?'

'Neither.' I stopped and watched as she removed the gloves. She was wearing an inner on her left hand but nothing on her right.

'Fair enough,' I laughed.

'Four for not many, Toby Jones,' Scott said, smacking me on the back as he passed me. 'Game on, mate.'

'Your new friend?' asked Ally.

'When you're playing for Australia with a common goal, anything's possible.'

We had them 4–55. The game was probably evenly balanced. Freddy was in and playing solidly.

Marty told us we had ten minutes before he wanted to chat with us.

'Where's Jimbo?' I asked him, helping myself to a sandwich.

'That's what I was about to ask you.' He looked annoyed.

'I'll go upstairs and have a look.'

'Back in ten, Toby. Jimbo or no Jimbo.' I nodded in agreement. We had a big game to win, and if it had to be done without Jimbo then so be it.

Although I hadn't seen any Grubbers on the field, an uneasiness had been gnawing away at me with every minute of Jimbo's non-appearance and it only grew as I bounded up the escalators and ran along the corridor to the corporate box that we had called home this past week.

'Jimbo?' I called, flinging open the door. There was no answer. All his clothes and belongings were still lying haphazardly about the room, just as they had been that morning. I flung open cupboard doors, searched under the portable beds and poked my head into the bathroom further down the corridor. Nothing.

Something someone had said, some comment that had been made, was making me feel nervous, but for the life of me I couldn't recall just what it was. Was it one of the coaches who had said something?

I returned to our room and gazed out over the ground. Marty and one of the other coaches were talking with two of our players down by the fence.

There was no way Jimbo would miss this match of his own choosing. Something or someone had taken him. A Grubber? That was the only explanation. I looked at my watch. Two minutes.

'I'll find you, Jimbo,' I muttered, closing the door gently. I wasn't exactly sure how, but it was going to have to wait until after the last session of play. I knew Jimbo wouldn't want me missing it.

12 What a Finish

Sunday — afternoon

'Do you think they'll go for the outright?' I asked Marty.

'I think they'll try and not lose any wickets for the first half hour and just see where they stand. As I said to the team, Toby, the first eight overs are critical. If we can get a wicket, maybe two, we really have the upper hand. They've got a long tail. Attack, attack.'

'And we can't get an eleventh player?'

Marty shook his head. 'We're lucky to have your friend Ally out there. It's only that her father was here and was able to sign an indemnity form.'

'Her dad's here?'

'He's called Peter,' he said, giving me a wink. 'Looked a lot like your old man actually.'

'You mean Dad —'

'Keep your shirt on, Toby. We made all the phone calls. Now go and lead your team out onto the MCG and don't come back until we've scored a famous Ashes victory.'

I jogged down the steps, adjusting my green cap, Scott close behind me. Dad must have signed for Ally to make it legit for her to play, though I doubt he would have done it without her parents knowing.

'How many more overs have you got in you, Scott?'

'Plenty. Don't take me off. I'll bowl unchanged from the far end.' A bank of dark clouds had moved over the ground; the air was thick and humid.

'There might be some swing out here. Keep the ball off the ground and shiny,' I called.

The first six overs were uneventful, with one half chance going just over second slip off a nice outswinger from Scott. The four that resulted hurt almost as much as the missed chance; it was their first boundary for ages.

'We need to suck them in for easy runs,' I said to Scott at the end of his over.

For my next over I had two slips, a gully, third man and a short straight mid-off on the off-side. I'd left a massive gap out through the covers — hopefully to tempt the batters to try and hit the ball out there but with an angled bat. On the on-side I had a fine leg, mid-wicket and mid-on. It was amazing how much you missed having the full team of eleven players to use.

The England batter played the first two balls crisply to Scott at short mid-off. I pitched the third ball slightly wider. He couldn't help himself; he swung wildly at it carving the ball out past point for four.

I bowled the next ball slightly quicker, but on the same line as the previous ball. Again he went for it, but this time only managed to get a thick edge. I held my breath as the ball flew to Barton in the gully. He took the catch in front of his face and hurled the ball into the sky.

'That's the one,' Scott yelled, as we came together to congratulate Barton. He'd taken a blinder.

I brought Jaimi from mid-wicket in to a bat pad position for the new batter. I sensed everyone on their toes as I charged in to bowl to the England keeper.

It was a short, rearing delivery. The keeper went to duck but left his bat dangling in the air. The ball crashed into the handle, lobbing towards Jaimi. He snatched at it, but only managed to flick the ball into the air. Before he could grab the rebound, the batter gave the ball a little flick with his bat, tapping it away from Jaimi's outstretched fingers.

It was an instinctive reaction, but we all appealed. The umpire nodded his head then raised his finger in the air. You weren't allowed to hit the ball twice, but worse, he had obstructed the fielder.

'Do you get the wicket?' Scott asked, as we came together again. I shrugged. I didn't care.

'Team hat-trick,' I said. We watched the new batter walk slowly to the crease.

'It's that tall all-rounder. Give him another bouncer,' Scott said.

'I agree. Let's crowd around him.' Barton was rubbing his hands together in anticipation. But I had another plan.

'Yorker,' I whispered to Ally. Exactly the ball he hopefully wasn't expecting. The last ball crashed into his feet then ricocheted onto the base of his off-stump. For a ghastly moment I thought the bails weren't coming off, but then one of them toppled over and fell to the ground.

'Ball must have slipped,' I grinned at Scott, who was staring at me in amazement.

'Yeah, right. I would have gone the yorker too,' he said, nodding his approval. We cleaned up the tail quickly, Scott bagging the last three wickets. The England players lined up and shook our hands as we left the ground.

There were speeches and presentations and it wasn't until just after five that Ally, Rahul and I were finally able to get away.

'So what's going on?' Ally asked, as they followed me upstairs to the corporate box. I was still on a high after the game and especially after receiving the small trophy for being nominated player of the match, but knew that some fast thinking had to be done. We were told that the ground would be closing in an hour and that all players, parents, friends and supporters had to be out by seven o'clock.

'Georgie is with Jim at the Timeless Cricket Match,' I said. 'She was taken by a Grubber.'

'A Grubber?' Rahul looked confused. I explained

to them everything that had happened as I hurriedly packed my gear.

'Is she safe?' Ally asked.

'She's with Jim, so yes, she's safe.'

'Especially now that the Father Time guy has been stitched up,' said Rahul. I glanced over at him. 'What?' he asked.

'No,' I said, shaking my head. 'You're right.' I didn't want to share my doubts about what had happened at the scoreboard. 'She should be okay. It's Jimbo that I'm worried about.'

'What do we say to Georgie's mum now?' asked Ally, helping me with my cricket kit.

'And Jimbo's parents?' Rahul added.

'Come on, Rahul,' Ally said, taking him by the arm. 'I think Toby's got enough problems to sort out. We'll think of something.'

'Thanks, guys.' They paused at the door. 'And thanks for helping out there.' I jerked my thumb at the window to indicate the ground behind me.

'Hey, well played yourself.' Ally stepped forward and gave me a quick hug. 'You look worried, Toby. Relax, things will sort out. They always do with you and Jim.'

'If only he was here,' I muttered.

13 Toby meets Toby

Sunday — evening

It was strange being home again after the enormous excitement of the cricket camp and Ashes Test at the MCG. I moped around the house, feeling removed; almost as if I wasn't a part of the family.

Mum and Dad must have realised the huge letdown I was going through after such an exciting week and left me to myself. They didn't even ask about Jim, assuming he was with friends. I'd mentioned that he'd met some at the library.

Finally I hauled myself off the bed, pushed aside the cricket magazine I'd been skimming through and went down to say goodnight to everyone.

'Great news about the cricket camp,' Mum beamed, dropping the tea towel she was holding and giving me a warm hug.

'The cricket camp? You mean the award?'

'What award, sweetie?' she said. Dad looked up from the kitchen table. I felt my stomach lurch. The

122

clock on the kitchen wall told me that time had just gone backwards about three and a half hours.

'But I've *been* to the cricket camp,' I said slowly, looking from Mum to Dad.

'In your dreams, Toby,' Dad laughed as he stood up. 'And I suppose you got to play on the MCG itself?'

I rushed out of the room, for some reason suddenly thinking about Jim and whether he would be alive right now. I stopped dead as soon as I entered the hall. Barely a metre away from me was myself, talking on the telephone! Hearing Dad follow me out into the corridor, I dashed into the laundry, gently closing the door. My heart was thumping. What was happening? I could hear myself talking to Jimbo. They were the exact words I'd used over a week ago.

I'd travelled back in time, but how? And why wasn't I being forced into my other self? How long would I be here, a week behind my real self? I racked my brain, trying to recall whether I'd felt anything a week ago when I'd made the call to Jimbo, but there was nothing I could remember.

Then I realised that Jim would be here. I pressed my ear to the door, but could hear nothing. Easing the door open, I peered around the edge. There was no one in sight. Carefully I stepped into the corridor, looking left then right.

What would happen if Mum or Dad saw two Tobys?

'Toby! You did it!' Natalie screamed, rushing to hug me.

'Hi, Nat,' I said quietly. 'Thanks.'

'Why are you whispering?' she asked, cocking her head to one side.

'It's hard to explain. It's sort of a game.'

'Cool, can I play?'

'Yeah, sure. But first, where's Jim?' She looked at me oddly.

'Silly, you were talking to him just a moment ago.' Suddenly she spun around and ran towards the front of the house.

'Natalie?' I cried, wondering what had set her off like that. 'Natalie?' A wave of nausea spread up through my stomach. Stumbling forward, I fell to my knees, clutching my sides ...

'Everything all right, Toby?' Dad called. I opened my eyes. I was lying on my bed. He came into the room. 'Toby?'

'Yes,' I croaked, relieved to be back in my own room. 'Dad?'

'Yes, Toby?'

'The cricket camp was great.' I watched his face nervously, but he merely smiled.

'You were fantastic,' he said. Letting out a long, thankful sigh, I rolled over, desperately hoping that there would be no more sudden travels.

But only a few hours later it happened again.

My mind flashed back to what Jim had said about Father Time and his ability to move people around from the present to the past; and possibly the future too. Was that what was happening to me? Had Father Time escaped his scoreboard prison?

124

* * *

I found myself waking up in the front garden. Someone was calling my name. I almost answered, but stopped myself just in time as a young Toby came running around the corner and up the front steps. He stopped suddenly and turned to me. I froze.

'Who are you?' he asked. My mouth went dry. I was looking at myself as a five- or six-year-old.

'I'm Toby,' I said. It was the first thing to come into my head. His face lit up.

'Mum!' he called.

'No, wait!' I said, reaching out a hand. He edged away from me. The door behind him opened. I swung around quickly and ran to the shed, then raced down the side before scrambling over the fence. Had Mum seen me? I slouched against the side of the fence, waiting for someone to arrive, but no one came.

In spite of the warm sun I shivered, finally closing my eyes as I rested my head against the fence. When I woke I was lying in bed. I sat up quickly, turning to glance at the clock. 3.34 a.m.

If I could just get through the night, I thought, switching on the light. Maybe if I could stay awake, I could also stay in my own time. I pulled down my album of cricket and football cards and grabbed a couple of magazines and the novel I was reading.

Slowly I worked my way through the album of cards, trying to memorise the players and their numbers. My eyes felt heavy as I turned another page.

'Ricky Ponting,' I muttered, yawning. 'Number four. Michael Clarke, number five.' The cards blurred. 'Michael Hussey ...'

I woke up with the card album lying across my chest. I looked at the clock. 8.45 a.m. 'Yes!' I shouted, pushing the album aside and jumping out of bed. I raced down to the kitchen.

'Dad?'

'In here.' His voice was tense. 'Hurry!' I walked quickly into the living room.

'Oh my God,' Mum gasped, resting a hand on Dad's shoulder. 'I had no idea.'

'What is it?' I cried, sitting down in front of the television.

Dad held up a hand for me to be quiet. I turned to the television.

'He was just sitting in the meeting here. In this chair,' a woman was saying. She paused, stifling a sob. 'Then he simply disappeared. I saw it. I mean I saw him go. I don't think anyone else did.'

A narrator's voice took over.

'All over the world, similar stories are unfolding. Contact is desperately being sought with any Test cricketer, but at this stage none have been found. The same terrible fate appears to have beset female Test cricketers. Reports from New Zealand, where the women's Test team was practising for their upcoming tour of India, suggest that most of the training squad has disappeared. Melanie Riley has more.'

I slumped down in the chair in shock as the reporter's face filled the screen.

'It appears that only the squad members who have actually played Test cricket have disappeared,' she said, breathlessly. 'Although none of the remaining players or officials would speak to us, it would seem that there is no indication of a kidnapping or ransom situation.'

'Good God,' Dad sighed, shaking his head.

'Dad?'

He turned to look at me. 'Every person who has ever played Test cricket has vanished,' he said.

'Vanished?' I asked.

He rubbed his eyes wearily. 'I've been watching since just after six this morning. Gone. Every one of them.' His voice was choked and I thought he was going to cry.

'But how? Where? Where have they gone to?'

He shook his head again. 'No one knows. Every Test cricketer, past and present,' he mumbled. I froze. Past and present. And future? Jimbo! I almost said his name aloud. 'He'll play Test cricket one day.' Wasn't that what one of the coaches had said about him?

'Scott,' I muttered, rushing to the phone. Was he gone too? And Cam? And yet I was still here? Did that mean that I wasn't going to play Test cricket?

Frantically, I searched the phone book for Scott's number. There were only three Cravens. I dialled, not sure whether I wanted him to be there or not. The phone was engaged. I tried again a few minutes later.

'Hello?' a tired voice said.

'Is Scott there?'

'Who is this?' the woman said, suddenly alert.

'Sorry, it's Toby. Toby Jones. I was wondering if I could speak to Scott.'

'You haven't heard?' Her voice was flat. I felt my skin prickle. So Scott had gone too. A future Test cricketer. But gone where?

'I'm sorry, Mrs Craven. I didn't know.'

'No, well we haven't heard from him since last night. He wasn't in any sort of trouble, was he?'

'Trouble?'

'At the camp. Did he upset someone? I know he's not the most easily managed boy, and he does have a very short fuse.'

I apologised again, adding that if I heard anything I'd ring her straight away. Mrs Craven gave me her mobile number and I jotted it down.

'I'll come back for breakfast in a minute, Mum,' I yelled. I headed back to my bedroom and got dressed, checking that the scorecard and cricket ball were safely tucked away in a pocket of my shorts, and then sat down on my bed. Jimbo. Scott. Who else had gone? Right across Australia kids would be missing. Babies? Was there a baby only just born, a future Test cricketer, who had recently vanished?

A sick feeling swept through me. Had I somehow caused all this? Burying my head in the pillow, I screwed my eyes shut, willing it all to be just some horrible nightmare.

* * *

'Aren't you a bit young to be here?' said a voice. I looked up. A tall boy wearing a black suit stared down at me. I was in some sort of hall, surrounded by streamers and balloons and senior kids talking and dancing. I scanned the faces, searching for someone I recognised. Then I froze.

On the far side of the hall, standing talking to a girl I recognised, was myself — but older; maybe three or four years older. I was in the future. For the first time ever I had travelled forward. Jim had told me that this would never happen, and yet I was certain that I was staring at an older me. And the girl I was with was Lisa. Lisa! A nice enough girl who I'd known since Year 2, but had never really spoken to in all that time. Why her? What about Georgie? Or Ally?

I moved forward into the main part of the hall, searching for more kids I could recognise. Many of the faces were new to me. Maybe I'd changed schools? Maybe I was living in a different town? A different country?

And then I saw Ally, dancing closely with a guy I didn't recognise. She looked beautiful. She was wearing a long, shiny red dress.

'Ally?' I said, moving closer. She maintained her close hold on the boy but turned her eyes towards me. I sensed her stiffen. She whispered something to the boy, who shrugged and moved away quickly. 'Ally, it's me. Toby.'

She glanced nervously across the room. I followed her gaze to the older me.

'Toby?' she whispered. 'But ... but ...' Her voice faded.

'I've come forward in time. From our time.'

'What do you mean, *our* time? This is my time.'

I shook my head, confused. I didn't want this conversation. 'Ally, what happened? What happened to all the Test cricketers? Did they return?' I held my breath, dreading her reply. She stared at me sadly. My heart plummeted.

'No. They were never found. Not one.'

'And Jimbo?' She shook her head.

'But you know all this, Toby. You're standing over there. You —'

'No! Don't tell me anything,' I said quickly. I didn't want to hear any more. Not about me. But I had to ask about Jim. I felt in my pocket for the scorecard. It was still there. 'Ally?' I whispered. She leant forward to hear. 'What about Jim?' I could tell straight away from the grim expression on her face that the news wasn't good. I turned away, conscious of the tears welling up.

'Toby, what will you do?' she asked.

I took a deep breath. 'I have to get to the MCG and place the scorecard in the first *Wisden*.'

'Now?'

I nodded. Ally noticed me staring at Lisa and my older self.

'You changed so much,' she said softly. Suddenly

130

she grabbed me by the shoulders. 'Hey, it seems okay that the two of you are in the room together.'

'Yeah, so?'

'Well, the big Toby over there can drive you to the MCG!' she squealed, clapping her hands together.

'No, wait!' I called, but Ally had already left me. I edged back towards a table covered in drinks and watched Ally talking with Toby. Lisa was not looking happy. For a moment I thought my older self wouldn't even come. He appeared reluctant, even after glancing in my direction. Finally he ambled over, a few steps behind Ally.

'Toby, meet, um, Toby,' Ally said. I stared at my older self as he stared at me, his face slowly turning white.

'Oh my God,' he whispered finally. 'It's happened.'

'What's happened?'

'Have you got the scorecard?' he asked, pulling out a bunch of keys from his trouser pocket. I nodded.

'We need to get —' we both said simultaneously. I smiled, reaching out a hand, but Toby flinched.

'No,' he said. 'Not too close. Let's go.'

'I'm coming too,' Ally cried, running after us. 'Oh, you were *so* cute,' I heard her say quietly to Toby. He screwed up his face but didn't reply.

'Is this your car?' I asked, staring at the shiny red hatch. I had a hundred questions to ask, but I sensed that the older Toby wasn't going to be telling me much.

'Not exactly,' he said, unlocking the doors. While Toby concentrated on the drive through the city to the MCG, I stared out the window, sitting perfectly still and praying that I wouldn't suddenly disappear back to my own time.

'You got a plan for getting in?' Toby asked, turning around while we waited at a set of red lights.

'David?' I suggested. 'Can we ring him? I know he lives close by.'

'He'll never get there by himself,' Toby muttered, taking a mobile phone out of his jacket pocket. 'Number's in there.' He passed it to me. I found the number and dialled.

'Why won't he meet us there? This is really important.'

'Toby, David's in a wheelchair. He's paralysed,' said Ally. 'There was an accident.'

'What? How?' I gasped. Suddenly I could hear David talking on the phone.

'Hello, David Howie?'

'David, what happened?' I said.

'I beg your pardon? Who is this?'

'It's Toby Jones. Remember?'

'Here, give that to me.' Toby snatched the phone out of my hand.

'David, sorry. Um, yeah it's me. Toby. Something big has come up. We ... I need to get into the library.' I leant forward, trying to hear the conversation. 'Frank?' Toby said. He nodded a couple of times. 'Yep.' He turned to Ally. 'Here, get this number

132

down.' Ally grabbed a piece of paper and pen from the glove box and wrote down the number Toby called out. 'Okay, David. I'll ring you in the morning.' There was a pause. Toby was looking anxious. 'Um, how are you anyway?' he asked. 'Oh, that's good. Great.' A moment later he rang off.

'What happened to David?' I asked. 'Why is he in a wheelchair? You've got to tell me.' I noticed the strained look on Toby's face. Finally Ally turned around in her seat.

'He had an accident. He slipped and fell down a flight of stairs.'

'Where? How?'

'Oh Jesus, does it matter?' Toby snapped, thumping the steering wheel with his hands.

'You did it,' I said, slowly. 'I did it!'

'Yes. We did it. You know how he's always rushing about that place, the library at the MCG ... carrying things.' Toby's voice petered out.

'When?' I asked, an idea forming in my head.

'Does it matter?' he said, angrily.

'Yes! It does,' I shouted at the back of his head. I didn't like the guy behind the wheel. Not one bit. And yet it was me. Ally reached out and clasped my wrist gently in her hand. She smiled, shaking her head briefly. Perhaps she would tell me later.

We travelled in silence until Toby turned into a large car park behind the Members Stand. The MCG hadn't changed much since my time, though it looked like some of the trees were missing from the grassy areas and more paths criss-crossed the car parks. While Toby spoke again into his mobile phone, I felt Ally's hand briefly take mine. A piece of paper passed between us; I shoved it into my pocket and followed her to the entrance.

'Toby Jones?' a security guard called, suddenly appearing from our left.

'Frank?'

'Come on. I don't know what you're up to here with your girlfriend and little brother, but if it's okay with David, then it's okay with me.'

We followed him through the eerie half light of the MCG, down corridors and up stairs.

'Here,' Ally whispered in my ear.

'The accident?' She nodded briefly then moved up alongside Toby, who flinched as she put her arm through his. 'Idiot,' I muttered. What had happened? Why was I with Lisa and not Ally?

We arrived at the library doors. Frank looked at us suspiciously.

'You really are Toby Jones, right?' he said, looking doubtfully at Toby.

'Yes, now can you hurry? We're missing out on the Year 12 social.' I kept my face down, as Frank grunted and unlocked the door.

'Wait here while I turn off the alarm.' The interior of the library was dark except for pale shafts of light coming from the windows to the right. I glanced along the glass cabinet, my eyes searching the spines of the *Wisden*s.

'We need the keys for the *Wisden* cabinet,' I said. Toby didn't turn around.

'All right,' Frank called from inside.

'Where are they?' Toby said, stepping into the main section of the library. He whistled softly, looking around as if he hadn't been here in ages. I ran my eyes along the *Wisden*s — 2006, 2007, 2008, 2009 . . .

'It's 2010,' I breathed, shivering.

'Did you hear me?' Toby was staring at me.

'Um, on his desk. Top drawer.' Toby disappeared into David's office, returning a moment later with a bunch of keys.

'Here,' he said. I took them from him, recognising the *Wisden* cabinet key straight away. There was a soft click as I turned it in the lock.

'This will change everything,' I whispered, relieved that the first *Wisden* was here. I pulled it down off the shelf carefully. Unlike the *Wisden*s I knew, this one was a papery edition; a sort of soft orangy pink, with lots of writing on its cover. It looked and felt old and valuable.

I held the scorecard in one hand and slowly moved it towards the open book. I could think of nothing to say. Ally hadn't moved from the entrance. I looked up into Toby's eyes. 'Why are you with Lisa?' I asked finally. The older Toby looked at me sadly.

'If only you knew.' There was a whooshing sound and I was gone.

'Toby?' My voice was lost in a frenzy of haze and mist. Some invisible force was pressing my body from all sides, squeezing me. Then just as suddenly the pressure was released and I felt myself floating down, down until my head nestled thankfully into something soft. For a moment I lay there, too frightened to move. The familiar smell of bed had never seemed so good. My fingers were curled gently around the scorecard which was resting in my hand. It had travelled back with me.

I lay awake in bed with the doona drawn tight over my shoulders, trembling despite the warm night.

Somehow — perhaps because of the future travel and the fact that I was able to insert the scorecard into the first *Wisden* —my understanding of what had happened was becoming clearer. As night slowly turned to morning, it dawned on me that the man in the scoreboard I had been talking to wasn't Jim; it was Father Time.

What else had he said that sunny afternoon as we sat together at the MCG? Had it only been two days ago? The power of Father Time. Able to distort the time of anyone he comes into contact with? I had just been the autumn leaf — going forward and backwards in time. How long might it have gone on for had Jim not told me to put the scorecard into the *Wisden*?

I was surprised at how calmly I was taking on board this new knowledge. It was as if I was a watcher, not directly involved in proceedings. Was this another hidden talent possessed by Cricket Lords? Perhaps it was just tiredness, deadening my emotions and fears.

What did Father Time need? The scorecard, a copy of the first *Wisden*?

I must have drifted off to sleep again. I awoke to the gentle sound of someone tapping. There was only one person who knocked like that. I burst out of bed and rushed to the door, then froze. Jim or Father Time? My senses were alive and tingling. The calmness of earlier had vanished, replaced by a cold hard lump of jittery nerves, prodding me in the base of my stomach.

'Who is it?' I called, trying to make my voice sound steady.

'Toby, my dear boy. It's Jim.'

'Jim? Is it really you?' I opened the door slowly. He stood there smiling, his arms outstretched. I didn't move.

'Toby, it's all right —'

'Where's Georgie?' He seemed momentarily taken aback.

'Georgie is still in the scoreboard.' I looked carefully into his eyes, trying to detect any sign at all that this wasn't Jim, but there was nothing about his appearance that indicated Father Time's spirit was inside him now. Had Father Time's possession of Jim now had enough time to be complete and therefore undetectable? 'I need the scorecard, Toby. I need —'

'NO!' I shouted. 'You gave me the scorecard. You said I was to look after it. Not to give it to anyone.' His eyes flashed black and a shadow passed over his face. I shivered. The room had gone suddenly cold. The tingling in my stomach had become a grinding pain.

'Don't be foolish, Toby. Georgie is your friend. Your best friend. Her life is in danger.'

'You're not Jim.' I backed away; suddenly horrified that Father Time himself was standing here in my home. The man took a step forward. The door closed behind him — on its own.

'You're a smart boy, as the old man warned me.' He was slowly moving towards me. 'But your time of tricks and escapades is over. The Timeless Cricket Match has resumed. I have at my disposal every player who has played Test cricket and is to play. Once the scorecard is destroyed, I and I alone will be the only being travelling through time.'

'I'll never give it up. I'll destroy you first!'

The man in front of me stood still and laughed softly. 'You see, Toby Jones, therein lies your problem. For if you destroy me, you destroy any chance of the old man passing on his wisdom and knowledge about time travel to you. And where will that put *you*? I'm not sure that you'd survive.'

Someone was moving in the corridor outside. Should I call out? As if sensing my thoughts, the figure of Jim suddenly vanished. The curtains billowed slightly and I felt a rush of cool air. He had gone.

14 The Battle with Father Time

Monday — afternoon

There was only one place he could have gone. It was where Georgie was; it was where maybe all the Test cricketers were. He knew I'd follow. This was it. I felt light, detached; as if it wasn't me moving quickly around my room, getting the scorecard from beneath my pillow, putting on a change of clothes, picking up the cricket ball. A sense of calm had taken over. There was a job to do and I knew with a crystal clear clarity that there was only one person who could do it.

'You're off again?' Mum said, walking past my room on her way into the kitchen.

'Things to do, you know.'

She laughed. 'Since when does a boy on holidays have *things* to do?' I shrugged, grabbing an apple and a snack bar from the cupboard. 'Is that breakfast?' she asked.

'I won't be long, Mum.' Walking out the front door, I wondered how close my prediction would be to the truth.

No one was answering at Ally's house when I phoned but Rahul was home when I tried him.

'Rahul, I need a favour,' I said quickly. 'I'm on my way round, okay?'

'Sure, Toby. Have you heard?' We chatted on the phone about the disappearances while I rode to his house. It took fifteen minutes, so by the time I arrived Rahul knew as much as I did about Jim, the missing cricketers and my plans. There wasn't much to tell about my plans. I had my cricket ball and not much else except any power I had as a Cricket Lord.

'I've got a *Wisden* ready,' Rahul said, meeting me in his front garden. We walked around to a secluded area of shrubs and bushes.

'Thanks, Rahul.'

'Will you return to this spot?'

'Will I return, more to the point. Find a zero. Anywhere. It doesn't matter.'

Rahul opened the new *Wisden* in his hands and flicked through some pages. 'Here we go,' he said. 'There's plenty on this page.'

'Australia must have been bowling,' I said, trying to lighten the mood.

'They were.' For a moment I thought he was going to give me all the details of the match.

'Don't forget to let go as soon as my finger touches the zero, okay?'

'Of course.' Rahul guided my finger to the spot. The zero flew out at me so quickly from the messy swirl of numbers and letters that I almost looked away. But I held my gaze and an instant later I felt the familiar chill of my new surroundings cool my flesh.

I never arrived in the same place, and I sensed straight away I was some distance from the cricket ground. Perhaps the faster you travelled to get here, the more removed you were from the Timeless Cricket Match.

I took a moment to get my bearings. Like last time, worn tracks wound their way through the dry and dead terrain. I followed the main track, occasionally stooping and ducking to avoid sharp overgrown branches jutting out over the path. At one point it got quite dark, but I pressed on. What choice did I have?

From the distance, some way ahead of me, came a sound I hadn't heard before. It was a soft kind of rumble. It was the noise of a crowd, though no one was cheering. It was the sound of a hundred voices; maybe a thousand. Quickening my pace, I wondered if the noise could be the terrified voices of all the lost cricketers.

This time it was a short, steep climb up a barren path that brought me into view of the cricket ground. I was coming in from behind the scoreboard and for a few moments all I could see was its broad, wooden back. But as I climbed the small hill, my eyes took in the huge stand to its left.

I stopped dead. It was full to bursting with people, colourfully dressed people. People of all shapes and sizes: babies, toddlers, children, young adults and the elderly. Most of them were sitting down.

A line of Grubbers paced up and down in an area between the bottom of the stand and the ground. Were they guards, keeping everyone in place?

The noise from the ground became a dull, thunderous roar as I got closer to the oval. It was a strange mixture of wailing and shouting; I could hear loud and animated conversation mingled with cries of despair and anguish. The stand was overflowing with people. They spilled out into a smaller open stand, further away to the left, and there were still more people bunched in tightly on wooden benches that ran around the entire half of the oval.

'Quite a sight, Toby Jones!' a harsh voice called from above. Jim's face peered through one of the scoreboard slats. And then another head appeared.

'Georgie!' I cried, rushing towards the ladder.

'If you want her life spared, then bring me the scorecard.'

'What about everyone else?' I shouted. I'd reached the stairs. I stumbled upwards, blind panic taking over the bolt of fear that had initially gripped me when I'd heard Father Time's raspy voice.

'Let go of her,' I cried, bumping my way across the first level and reaching the next set of stairs. They were on the third level. I rushed past two Grubbers who paid me no attention at all. They were concentrating on the scoring.

Finally I reached the top level. The figure of Jim stood with his arms folded, his back to the openings on the face of the scoreboard and the ground beyond.

'You can't —'

'Silence!' he bellowed. The old scoreboard shook as his voice echoed into every corner of the wooden room. 'I have been watching you for some time, Mr Jones. You are very nearly the last Cricket Lord left and thus are going to perish like the rest of them.' He tossed his head, indicating the crowd outside. 'But, as a Cricket Lord myself, I am capable of respect. It's your choice. Give me the scorecard and your life is saved. You simply remain here in the scoreboard for the rest of time, scoring the match.'

'Where's Jim?' I cried.

'Slipping further and further away. Every time you speak to me, Toby Jones, you give me strength and power to take over the old man's body more completely. Every word you utter pushes him further and further away. Talk to me, Toby Jones.'

I'd had enough. I made a dash for Georgie, who had been standing as though in a trance, looking blankly from me to the figure of Jim. Suddenly she started moving, walking towards me like a zombie.

'You really don't get it, do you?' Father Time snarled. Georgie's speed increased. I swerved at the last moment as she came hurtling towards me before smashing herself into the front of the scoreboard.

'Georgie!' I screamed, rushing to her. Some invisible force was lifting her off the floor. Reaching up I managed to grab onto her jacket. I held on grimly, feeling my own feet slowly rise from the wooden floorboards.

'Give me the scorecard and save your friend.'

'Georgie, wake up,' I pleaded, ignoring the voice. As my hold on her loosened, my fingers closed around something round and hard in her pocket. The material of her jacket slipped through my fingers but I clasped the object firmly in my left hand, turning my body to conceal my find. Was it a magic cricket ball like mine?

I spun round and hurled it at the figure of Jim. A roar of pain filled the tiny room. He staggered back, his eyes wide with shock. Behind me I heard Georgie's body collapse to the floor.

Taking out my own cricket ball, I ran towards Father Time. But I didn't notice the black square of wood flying towards me. It crashed into my hand as I went to release the ball and there was a loud crack as it connected with my wrist.

I gasped, reeling back in pain, and watched despairingly as the cricket ball fell to the floor and rolled slowly towards Father Time. Another wooden board flew towards me but I managed to duck just in time, feeling the wind as it whistled millimetres above my head and crashed into the wall opposite.

I lunged for Georgie's cricket ball, but just as my fingers grasped its edge, a foot crashed down on my wrist. The pain was excruciating. I was pinned to the ground.

'Stop this now,' Father Time said, but his voice was different. It was less harsh; softer. The ball had hurt him. As his hand reached down, searching for the scorecard, I rolled onto my back, kicking out with both legs with all the strength I had.

He staggered back slightly. It was all the time I needed. Quickly grabbing both the cricket balls, I hurled them simultaneously. The left arm throw was weak, my wrist throbbing and bruised, but he was still knocked backwards. His head hit the wall behind him, knocking a stack of wooden numbers to the floor. Dust billowed in a cloud over his head. Retrieving both balls, I got to my feet and moved towards him. His face — Jim's face — was twisted in pain, his black eyes staring at me with menace and hatred.

'I can toy with you as I like,' his voice quavered. My mind suddenly went blank. It was as if someone had removed my entire memory. All I knew was that I was in an old dusty room staring at an old man. I started to cry. A baby's cry; loud and piercing.

'What are you going to do now, Toby Jones? You're three years old and of no use to anyone.' A loud voice was shouting at me. I cried louder. 'Or shall we move ahead, hmm? Would you like that?'

The dust in my nose tickled but the sensation was taken over by an extreme burning pain in my hand. But that too disappeared as quickly as it had appeared.

I looked down in surprise and then dropped one of the balls in horror. My hand had suddenly become wrinkled and blotchy, covered in red and purple sores.

As I fell to my knees I just managed to release the ball from my right hand, but it was a lame throw — the throw of an old man. My withered arm felt like it was about to fall off with the effort.

'You're ninety years old and dying,' Father Time sneered. I held his gaze, sensing that he was uncomfortable with my stare. From behind me I could hear the faint sound of someone moving, but I was too tired to react. I was struggling to fight an overwhelming desire to just lie down and rest. To sleep forever. But somehow, from somewhere deep within me, a small voice was telling me to maintain eye contact with Father Time. Nothing else mattered.

New pains and aches were breaking out all over my body. My legs felt stiff and my arms were frail and useless, yet still I continued to stare into his evil black eyes. Slowly the Jim figure recoiled, stumbling backwards.

A sense of overwhelming power was pouring out of me. It was frightening, but it was having the desired effect. My skin started to prickle as I felt it gently pull and stretch, gradually returning to its normal smooth state.

'Toby!' a voice yelled. My concentration broken, I turned away from the Jim figure. A great cloud of white dust billowed around his head as he waved his arms. His body was jerking uncontrollably.

'Georgie? Is that you?'

'Where am I?' she shrieked. A terrifying gust of wind was spinning violently just above the Jim figure. Covering my head, I dived for the cricket balls as the ghostly image of Father Time reared over me. I could barely make out the shape of the twisted body as it spiralled in the air.

'Get out, Georgie!' I shouted, then hurled the fastest, hardest throw I could manage directly at Father Time's head. There was an explosion of sound as the ball connected; it then stopped in the space where his head had been. The spinning tornado was whipping up boards and chunks of wood, hurling them about the room in a frenzy of terrifying mayhem.

'Again, Toby,' I heard a voice call over the noise of the wind and a howling cry of anguish. The cricket ball was stuck in the spinning air, sucking the life out of Father Time. I hurled the other ball at the grey and black cloud as a plank of wood tore off the rear section of the wall, flying into the room.

More wood started to break away from the walls as the wind whipped around the room. My eyes stinging, I clung on to the frame of an open window overlooking the ground. I was hanging on grimly, my arms wrapped around the thin ledge of wood.

Outside, the crowd had gone silent; they were watching in amazement as the scoreboard was torn apart by this raging frenzy of ghostly wind. Even the cricketers and umpires on the field had paused.

I watched in horror as a section of roof blew clean away. Just when I thought I couldn't hold on any longer, the screaming sound stopped. Nervously I glanced around. Jim lay motionless on the floor, covered in dust and black blocks of wood.

'Georgie?' I whispered, slowly untangling myself from the window. Half the walls had disappeared along with most of the wooden numbers. 'Georgie, are you okay?' And then I saw her, lying on the ground at the foot of the scoreboard. One leg was angled awkwardly, bent and twisted.

'Nothing can be done,' a hoarse voice whispered from behind me. I spun around. 'I'm so sorry, Toby.'

'Jim!' I cried, rushing over to him. 'Is it really you?'

'Do not approach her, Toby. Do you understand?' I was surprised by the harshness in his voice, thinking suddenly that Father Time was still somehow dwelling in his frail body. But the cruelly twisted face was softer, gentler.

'But, Jim, is she all right?' He closed his eyes briefly. I turned away, but felt his weak grip squeeze my arm.

'Just promise me that you will not touch her,' he wheezed, then started coughing. Carefully I removed the blocks of wood and other debris that had half buried him.

'Jim, what's happened?' I choked, desperately trying to keep the tears of shock away. 'Jim?' I nudged him gently. He opened his eyes slowly, trying to focus on me. I took his hand and held it firmly. 'Come on, Jim. Tell me what to do.' He licked his dry lips.

'Toby,' he said finally, drawing me closer to him. His voice was barely a whisper. 'Only the guards are left. You must destroy the guards and free the cricketers.'

'But how?'

'Beneath the stand.' His voice was faltering.

'Jim?' I breathed, bending even closer. 'I can't leave you.'

'You must, Toby. I have one more journey to make.'

'Journey? Where?'

'Go, Toby. Go to the turnstile beneath the stand.' He paused again, catching his breath.

'Jim, will you be all right?' Again he ignored me.

'You will be asked a question, Toby. Answer the question and then ask for the cricket balls. Only then —'

'Jim?' I shook his shoulders, trying to rouse him. His breathing was laboured. 'Please, Jim, wake up.' His face looked suddenly peaceful. Easing my arm from beneath his head, I gently rested his head back on the floor.

'I'll be back,' I whispered, more determined than ever to finish what had to be done.

Grabbing the two cricket balls, I charged down the stairs, glancing quickly at the broken body of Georgie, lying limp and alone in a crumpled heap at the foot of the scoreboard. I forced myself to turn away, recalling the tone of Jim's words and his warning about not going near her.

15 Through the Turnstiles

Monday — afternoon

Tempted as I was to run straight to the throng of Test cricketers packed into and around the main stand, I realised that I had to first obey Jim's instructions.

I ran across a grassy bank, hardly noticing the ground beneath my feet. Yet again the game had paused, but the umpires and players were still on the field. The Grubbers who were guarding the Test players appeared agitated, running around and swooping menacingly over the frightened crowd.

Turning my head away, I sprinted across the slope unaware of the long arm and icy hand of a Grubber reaching out towards me as he came at me from my back. It was only when I heard the rush of air behind me that I realised he was on me.

There was a gurgling, choking sound as the Grubber penetrated into my body. Pressing the cricket ball into his chest, I mumbled the magic words, then stumbled and crashed to the ground. I could hear a sucking noise as I felt his being suddenly withdraw from my body.

I rolled over, sensing him coming at me again. As he dived on top of me, his face centimetres from mine, I thrust the ball hard into the air, again muttering the words. I felt the ball and my whole arm pierce his chest, going right through him. He shuddered and then collapsed in a heap beside me.

I watched in horror as his body materialised. The spirit was turning into flesh. In a matter of moments an old man was lying on the ground. Tentatively I touched his wrist, feeling for a pulse. His skin was clammy and cold; there was no life in him.

Fearing another attack, I got up quickly and sprinted on. The area behind the stand was deserted. A man wearing a grey coat stood at an entrance gate at the back of the main stand. I approached him warily.

'You cannot enter,' he said in a strange, vacant voice.

'I am Toby Jones,' I said, moving towards him. He appeared harmless enough, though he was a spirit, like the Grubbers.

'The Cricket Lord?' He looked at me for the first time. I nodded.

'What was the result of the fifth Ashes Test match of 1926?' Resting my hands on the cool iron turnstile, I closed my eyes. For a brief moment I panicked, wondering where the answer would come from, but then it was there; as if I'd known it all my life.

'England won by 289 runs.'

He didn't smile. 'Who made 120 for England at Trent Bridge in 196–'

'John Edrich,' I snapped, pushing at the metal bar. There was a click and suddenly I was inside the stand.

'About time too,' I thought I heard the man say. I spun around, suddenly remembering that I'd forgotten to ask about the cricket balls, but to my amazement he had vanished. Taking a few tentative steps, I glanced left then right. A Grubber was moving away from me to my left. I waited until he was out of view then headed in the opposite direction. Almost straight away I found myself in a narrow passage. As I followed it, I had the awful sense that someone was following, though whenever I turned, there was nothing behind me except an empty corridor. I pressed on another 20 metres, stopping when I saw yet another figure in a grey coat, standing outside a door. Just as I was about to call out I sensed movement ahead of me. I froze, edging back into the darkness of a small recess in the passage wall. A Grubber floated past. He paid no attention to the grey-coated figure, though surely he must have seen him. Were they partners after all? Was I being led into a trap?

I took a tentative step back into the corridor and turned to face the figure.

'I ... I —'

'The Cricket Lord?' Again the voice was soft and lilting.

'Yes,' I said, edging closer. 'Are you going to ask me another question?'

He smiled and shook his head.

'What about the Grubber?' he asked.

'He didn't see me,' I replied. The figure took a step to one side, reached around, opened the door behind him, and then, like the one I met at the turnstile, disappeared.

I entered the room quickly and stopped dead. It was like the Sanctum back at the MCG, the space inside totally out of proportion to the size it should have been. In the middle of the room was a chair and on the chair a note.

'Welcome, Cricket Lord,' it read. 'May your strength and courage win the day.' I glanced around. The wall to my left was lined with old wooden shelves and on the shelves were stacks of boxes. On the other side of the room was an old, dark green gate. I moved closer. 'The turnstile,' I breathed, touching its iron poles. Was this the gateway back to our time?

I turned around and rushed over to the shelves of boxes, tearing off the lid of one of them. Twelve neatly arranged shiny new cricket balls were nestled inside. Their newness seemed at odds with the run-down feel of the place.

I picked one up and knew straight away from the feeling it gave me that this was no ordinary cricket ball. There must have been hundreds of boxes. For the first time in ages I smiled. If I could just get these into the hands of the Test players upstairs in the stands, I thought, grabbing two of the boxes.

Hurling away the lids, I raced out into the corridor, almost colliding with a Grubber. Snatching one of the balls, I chucked it at him as hard as I could. The ball burst through him, smacking against the wall behind. The Grubber vanished in an instant.

'Beauty,' I whispered, picking up the ball. I turned and ran, and was straight away confronted by two more Grubbers. Two quick throws later they had vanished into thin air and the way ahead of me was clear again.

I arrived at the bottom of a huge set of wide wooden stairs. I could clearly hear a rumble of noise as I charged up the steps. I reached the top and gasped. The stand was packed with men, women and children. The air was filled with the sound of crying as adults tried to comfort young kids. I hadn't yet been noticed by any of the hundreds of Grubbers patrolling the aisles of the stand. I turned to the person next to me.

'Who are you?'

'Kerry O'Keeffe,' he said, staring at me quizzically. 'And when I wake up from this bloody nightmare I'll be a very relieved man.'

Kerry O'Keeffe. Australian leg spin bowler, 53 Test wickets, batting average of 25.76. The information poured into my head.

'G'day, Kerry,' I said, smiling. 'I've got a job for you.'

'If it means I don't have to talk to this old codger, then I'm all yours,' he said, bouncing up off his seat and moving away from the elderly cricketer next to him. 'Except for these blasted spooks,' he muttered, sitting back down again as a Grubber swept by. I shoved my hand that was holding the ball into the Grubber's stomach as he loomed up in front of me. There was a soft hissing sound and a moment later he disappeared.

'Here, take this box of balls. Throw them at the Grubbers.'

'The what?'

'The spooks,' I grinned. 'Go find anyone you think can throw a ball and get them to help you hit the spooks. With the cricket balls,' I added.

'It can't get any weirder,' Kerry mumbled, taking the box of balls from me.

There was no hope of finding Jimbo or Scott but I scanned the crowd anyway, desperately hoping I'd recognise someone. Finally my eyes came to rest on a familiar figure, a few rows down and away to my right.

'Freddy,' I gasped, moving towards him. He'd made it to Test cricket after all. 'Freddy!' I shouted. He glanced to his left, his face lightening suddenly. Kerry was already causing a commotion. He'd gathered together about six players or ex-players and they were carving their way through the army of

Grubbers down along the fence line. Many more people were standing up, wanting to join them.

Freddy was out of his seat and edging past a group of kids of similar age.

'What kept you?' he said, slapping me on the shoulder.

'Have you seen Jimbo or Scott?' I asked, grabbing his arm.

'Yeah, they're further over. Benny?' he called, turning back to where he'd been sitting. 'Go and get those two Aussie guys I was telling you about.'

'Meet us at the top of the stairs here,' I added. 'You guys, with us. Hurry!' The six kids who'd been sitting next to Freddy looked up at me nervously. 'Come on!'

'Do it!' Freddy added. I didn't wait to see if they were following. We needed more of the cricket balls.

'What's going on?' A man in a suit addressed me. His face looked familiar; I was sure I'd seen him on TV. There was a calm, confident air about him.

'We need to get everyone downstairs. First room on your left. There's a green turnstile in there. It will take everyone home,' I told him, remembering Jim's instructions. The look of bewilderment on his face quickly changed to amazement as a Grubber swooped up the stairs from behind him. Thrusting my arm out, I smashed the ghostly figure into oblivion right in front of the man's eyes.

'What shall I do?' he asked, staring around him, looking for the Grubber.

157

'Marshal everyone down these stairs and into the room below,' I said. 'But hurry. These Grubbers might change their minds about all of you.'

With the others following, I charged back down the stairs and into the turnstile room.

'Grab a box of balls each and take it upstairs,' I shouted, taking a box from the shelf and shoving it into Freddy's hands. 'Get anyone who can throw a ball to hit the ghosts!'

'With a cricket ball?' one of them asked, staring suspiciously at the box in his hands.

'Asani, it works. Believe me,' Freddy said, taking two boxes himself and rushing out. The others followed. I ran back to the door and was met by the guy in the suit. He was leading a line of men and women carrying babies and small kids.

'It's absolute chaos out there,' he grimaced. 'I hope you know what you're talking about.'

'This way,' I said, pointing to the metre-high turnstile.

'What is going on here?' the man said, aghast, staring at the structure.

'Trust me. This is the gateway.' And if it works, I thought, then at least I know Jim is his old self again, and not still being controlled by Father Time.

'What's he saying?' asked a woman who was carrying a tiny child, asleep on her shoulder.

'Um, did you come with the baby?' I said, as she stepped up to the turnstile.

158

'Of course I didn't. I've got no idea where I am or whose child this is and I can't find its mother.'

I took a deep breath.

'Listen, if I'm right, this turnstile here is going to take you back to the place you came from. You might end up in your place or you might end up in the child's place. I don't know. But you will be back.'

'By walking through this turnstile here?' She scoffed, turning to the man.

'I believe him,' the man said finally. 'It can't hurt.' Others in the line were pressing forward, wondering what was happening.

'Go!' I yelled, as two Grubbers swept into the room. I threw a cricket ball at the first one and he flew up into the air, crashing into the wall behind him. A quick-thinking guy further back in the line picked up the ball and flicked it at the other Grubber. He vanished into the air.

The woman with the baby stepped forward, carefully pushing the green rails forward as she walked through the turnstile. There was a click as the iron gate swung over and then she was gone.

'Oh my God,' said the man as an elderly guy stepped forward. We watched him gently push the metal gate. It clicked and he too vanished. 'Tony, come and supervise here!' the man shouted. 'Women, children and the elderly. Get them through.' The man glanced at me once more, nodded, then raced off.

'Hey, buddy, I want to stay and fight,' a guy said, grabbing me by the shoulder. He was the person who'd thrown a ball a few minutes ago.

'Great. We need to get all these boxes of balls upstairs,' I called. Together we gathered more boxes and raced back upstairs.

The scene we were confronted with was absolute chaos. There were people pushing and screaming. Word had spread quickly that there was an escape route downstairs and people were charging towards the exits. The spell of the Grubbers had been broken. Even as I watched, they were disappearing in droves, powerless to stop the onslaught of cricket balls being hurled with amazing accuracy at them.

'Order!' a man shouted. 'Stay calm, everyone.' His loud voice seemed to have the desired effect. I watched everyone shuffle slowly towards the stairwell. What if I was wrong? What if I was actually sending them to another place, even worse than this? Had Jim really spoken those words? Or had it been Father Time?

'Toby?' I spun around. Someone down near the fence was waving his arms frantically.

'Jimbo?' I battled my way through the throng of people all heading in the opposite direction. Scott was with him.

'We're getting out of here?' he asked. Relief swept over me.

'We are,' I said. 'You guys okay?'

'Better for seeing you,' Scott said, then grinned. 'I guess you never thought you'd hear me say that.'

I looked out at the ground. The players and umpires were standing with their arms folded, watching the action in the stand.

'Who are they?' Jimbo asked, standing next to me, staring out onto the oval. 'Do they talk?'

'All I know is that they're the spirits of past cricketers. And I think that's what everyone here was destined to become — a spirit. At some point in the future every person here in the stand would have gone out onto the ground to play cricket. That's what Father Time had organised,' I explained.

'And all these creepy ghost things that were guarding us?' asked Scott.

I looked at him. 'The same, except they were all waiting to play. They were frustrated, but harmless enough. They were waiting their turn to go and play out there.' I glanced over at the scoreboard. Wisps of smoke trailed from a couple of the openings. The area beneath it was littered with broken pieces of wood and other sections of the scoreboard. I felt an overwhelming urge to go to Georgie, whose lifeless shape I could just make out among the debris. I turned away, recalling Jim's words.

It took half an hour for the Grubbers to be eliminated. By then, a sense of calm and order had been restored as more and more of the past Test players organised everyone into lines that slowly wound their way up to the top of the stand, then snaked towards the room that held the turnstile. The stand had emptied completely and there was not a

Grubber to be seen. The only evidence of the battle that had just taken place were the hundreds of shiny red cricket balls that littered the stands and walkways. Some had made their way onto the actual oval. The old men were now slowly moving towards them. I watched as they gently tossed the balls back towards the fence.

'Come on, time to go,' I said, leading Jimbo and Scott up the main central aisle of the stand. We arrived at the turnstile room.

'We're going to do one last check of this God-forsaken place,' the suited man called. He and three others headed back out.

'Guys, I'm going back to the scoreboard,' I said.

'I'll come too, Toby,' Jimbo said. 'Scott?'

'Sure, man. I'm in.'

'No, I have to do this alone,' I said.

'Rubbish, Toby. You don't have to do anything alone. Come on.' We headed back upstairs, only to be stopped by the suited man.

'It's all clear,' he said. 'You boys can go —'

'John,' a man interrupted, joining us. 'There's an old guy up the back corner.'

'Well, why isn't he here?'

'He's passed away. Maybe a heart attack. But there's something —'

'Oh no,' I groaned, suddenly rushing back out. Was it Jim? My heart pounding, I charged up the stairs. 'Where is he?' I shouted. The others were just behind me.

'Over —' The man's voice froze. We looked in the direction of his pointing finger.

'Good Lord,' someone else breathed. As we watched, the guy who was slouched in the seat was slowly changing form. 'What's happening to him?' His body was fading in and out, disappearing then reappearing, but fainter each time.

'He's turning into a Grubber,' I said, finally turning away. 'Come on. There's nothing we can do.'

'Hey, where are you going?' the man asked.

'Leave him,' I heard the man in the suit say. 'That kid has saved everyone here today. He knows what he's doing.'

My thoughts turned to Jim and Georgie. What could I do to help them?

16 Caught!

With the others close behind me, I headed down the main stairs and onto the walkway that would lead us back to the scoreboard.

'What's that noise?' Jimbo asked, stopping suddenly. There was a strange banging and clattering coming from the scoreboard. I stopped dead too. It was only then I noticed that on the grass below, there were just a few pieces of wood and other material. There was no body.

'She's gone!' I cried, running towards the scoreboard.

'Who?' Scott asked, sprinting after me. We ran up the incline. A loud cry came from above.

'Toby!' Jimbo called. He had recognised Georgie's scream. We looked up. Her body appeared at one of the rectangular windows.

'Quick!' I yelled, rushing up to the scoreboard's edge as she fell through the opening. The others joined me, instinctively reaching their arms out as

Georgie plummeted through the air. She fell into our arms, the weight of her body sending us crashing to the ground. I heard someone groan. Slowly I opened my eyes, dazed and aching all over. Her foot had connected with the side of my head.

'Toby? You okay?' I watched through blurred eyes as Jimbo got up onto one elbow. 'Scott?'

'Bloody hell,' he said.

'Toby? Is that you?' Georgie whispered. I tried to sit up but fell back, a bolt of pain surging through my leg. But I couldn't wipe the smile from my face, and when Georgie pressed her hand into mine, I finally let the tears come.

I don't know how, or how long it took, but when I opened my eyes I was lying in my bed at home.

'Well, well. The hero awakes.'

'Jim?' I cried, sitting up. My head hurt and a wave of nausea swept over me; I slumped back down again.

'I'm afraid not, lad. It's only your father.'

'Dad? What happened?'

'Now that's a question that a lot of people are asking,' he said softly, running a hand gently through my hair. 'Every newspaper, news show and radio station wants a piece of you.'

'The cricketers have returned?'

'Every one of them plus all the other kids and babies that disappeared at the same time.' I closed my eyes and smiled. 'We did it, Jim,' I said under my breath. 'What about Jim?' I asked in a louder voice.

'No sign of him. I think you should —'

'Dad, I need a *Wisden*,' I said, slowly trying to sit up again. The pain in my head wasn't quite as sharp as before.

'Toby, now's not the time —'

'Dad, please. There's someone I want you to meet.'

'Toby, just lie back down —'

'The *Wisden*, Dad. It's just over there.' I pointed to the bookshelf.

'There's something you haven't been telling me, isn't there?' he said softly, getting up off the bed.

'How long have I been back?'

'Back?'

'Where was I? How did I get here?'

'Well, you and Georgie were found in Rahul's garden. You were unconscious and Georgie wasn't much better.'

'And the others? Jimbo?'

'They've all called. Even Scott.' I leant back against the pillow and sighed.

'Dad, I'm going to explain everything,' I said. 'I promise. But first, you've got to open the *Wisden*.'

'Which one?' It sounded like he was playing along with my game, humouring me to keep me happy.

'Any one. It doesn't matter.'

'Okay. You want me to read to you?'

'No. I want you to open it up to a scorecard.'

'Any scorecard?'

'Yes. Find a zero.'

'Well, there's plenty of those. Look at them all.' Dad held the book open for me.

'I can't see them, Dad.'

'What do you mean you can't see them? Is there something wrong with your eyes?' He came back to sit next to me, looking from me to the open page.

'Nothing, it's just that I can't ever see the writing in a *Wisden*.'

'Why on earth not?'

'Well, that's another thing I've got to explain to you. Where's the zero, Dad? Can you put my finger on it?'

'Sure, Toby.' He took hold of my hand and slowly guided my finger into the mysterious cloud of black and white.

'Dad, don't let go,' I said quickly, as a zero rose from the page.

The first thing I felt was warmth on my bare arms. For a fleeting moment I thought I must have come to the wrong place, but there in front of us, only 50 metres away, was the cricket oval. I'm not sure who was the more surprised. Dad just stood there, his mouth wide open, staring at the scene in front of him.

I was gawping too. The cold, grey, desolate place that had been the Timeless Cricket Match was now green and beautiful. There was a small scattering of people, sitting in the sunshine watching the game out in the middle.

Quickly I looked over to the scoreboard. It still looked old and run-down and had obviously been patched up in places, but there were no broken pieces of wood lying on the lush green ground below.

'Come on, Dad.' I took his hand and we ambled slowly away to our left.

'T-Toby, what's going on?'

'I'm going to let Jim explain all that,' I grinned. Gentle applause broke out around the ground. The batter had just stroked the ball neatly through the covers. I looked closely at the fielder chasing the ball, recognising him straight away. He was the old man whose body we had seen transform into a spirit. I glanced up into the stand; the place where he had been sitting was empty.

The thought suddenly occurred to me that at some long distant point in the future, I might be playing out there. Glancing at Dad's pale and anxious face I quickened the pace, hoping desperately that Jim would be where I left him; and alive too.

Ignoring Dad's gasps of surprise and wonder, I climbed the steps into the first level of the scoreboard.

'Jim?' My voice echoed around the bare wooden room.

'Toby?' Jim's voice rang out from the level above.

'C'mon, Dad,' I shouted, dragging him across the room. I let go his hand and flew up the stairs, rushing into Jim's outstretched arms. 'You're okay,' I said, as he held me close.

'As good as gold,' he beamed, looking me up and down. 'Peter!' Dad looked from me to Jim, astonishment written all over his face. 'Toby, why don't you score here while I take Peter upstairs and show him the sights?'

'Where's the old scorebook?' I asked, looking around for the table it had been on last time I was here.

'Ah, we have official scorers now,' he beamed. 'Over in the main stand. There have been a lot of changes around here, as you probably saw.'

'It's certainly a nice spot to be,' I agreed, turning to sit on a small chair. I looked out through an opening onto the ground below. Jim led Dad up the next flight of stairs. I had plenty of my own questions for Jim, but they were going to have to wait.

It must have been almost an hour later when Dad finally emerged, carefully descending the metal stairs.

'Of course I knew all along,' he said, walking slowly towards me. Jim was just behind him.

'Knew what? That I could time travel?'

'No, no. That you'll play Test cricket one day.' I glanced at Jim. He was smiling.

'Nothing is certain, Peter.'

'You can say that again,' Dad said. The three of us stood there for a moment in a comfortable silence.

'All the Grubbers have gone?' I asked Jim, looking back out the small opening towards the stand.

'All the bad ones, yes. And we have spectators slowly arriving so the Timeless Cricket Match is safe again.'

'And Father Time? He's gone too?'

'Thanks to you, Toby. He made a terrible mistake. His arrogance destroyed him.'

'What do you mean?'

'You remember up here in the scoreboard? He regressed you. I could see it happening through my own eyes yet I was powerless to do anything to stop him. But then he *aged* you, Toby. And that was his mistake.'

I recalled my gnarled and wrinkled hands and arms and the painful effort required to throw the cricket ball.

'Why?'

'You are a Cricket Lord, Toby, but a very young one. Your powers are nowhere near developed to their full potential. But when he aged you, suddenly he was confronted by all those years of wisdom and knowledge. Between the two of us, in those brief few minutes, we were able to overwhelm him.'

'But why didn't he just age me to death?'

'You are a Cricket Lord, Toby. It's not quite that easy.' I thought about the weird dreams I'd had as I'd moved forward and backwards in time. I mentioned them to Jim.

'Have I really been into the future?'

Jim smiled, slowly shaking his head. 'It is a future you won't recognise, Toby.'

'So it won't happen the way I saw it?'

'No, I believe not.'

'And Georgie? I thought she was dead.'

'For a little while there, she may well have been. But I waited.' Jim took out one of the wooden pieces, replacing it with another board.

'Waited?'

'I waited for you boys to return.'

'You mean Scott and Jimbo? You knew we'd come back?'

'Oh yes. When you've travelled around time as much as I have, Toby, you come to know all sorts of things that have happened or are going to happen.'

'And the Grubbers?'

'They wouldn't have harmed anyone.'

'But they attacked me and you.'

'That's true. We are Cricket Lords, and they knew that. As Cricket Lords we are also time travellers. We were vehicles for them to escape the Timeless Cricket Match and return to real cricket.'

'So that's why they didn't attack anyone else?'

'No. They were never meant to return.'

'But why didn't the Grubbers destroy the turnstile?'

'Because it never existed until you answered those questions.'

'From the guy in the grey coat?' I asked. Jim nodded. 'But —'

'Enough for now, Toby. It's time for you to take Peter home again. There is as much to do there as there is here.' Dad moved away from the opening.

'Will you come back with us?' I asked, already knowing the answer.

'Soon, Toby, but not yet.' He rested a hand on my shoulder, sensing my disappointment. 'Soon.'

Epilogue

Thursday — morning

For the next few days, the news was full of the events surrounding the strange disappearances. Jim had instructed Dad to keep me away from any media attention and I'd managed to make sure the others, including Scott, also gave nothing away. Officials at Cricket Australia, with the assistance of various people at the MCG and even David, were working overtime to keep things as calm as possible.

We returned to the MCG for a training session on Thursday morning. The first World Cup game was only two weeks away and although not all of the players were present, the workouts we had were intense and enjoyable.

Jimbo, Scott and I met Dad outside the Hugh Trumble Café at five o'clock, as arranged.

'How about we go up to the MCC library and say hi to David,' Dad suggested. Scott groaned. Although showered and changed, we were exhausted and hungry after the day's session. 'Come on, won't be for long.' Jimbo stared forlornly at the food behind the counter. 'You never know. You might even find some snacks in the library.'

'Yeah right,' Scott laughed, lugging his bag over his shoulder and following Dad. We headed off towards the library. 'Hey, isn't that him there?' Scott asked, pointing to a man at the top of the stairs balancing what looked like a tray of party pies on one hand and a jug of something in the other. I froze, knowing straight away what was about to happen. This was the time of David's accident. I had to stall, if only for a few seconds. I grabbed Scott's arm, crying out suddenly.

'What is it?' he said, turning sharply.

'Cramp,' I lied, clutching my leg. The others gathered in close. Dropping my kit, I stretched the leg out, glancing up to the top of the stairs. David hadn't noticed us and was walking slowly towards the library entrance. 'Phew, that's better,' I said. 'Sorry.'

'You sure?' Jimbo looked concerned.

'Yeah, I'm fine.'

'Damn it,' Scott sighed. 'I was gonna call out and get him to bring the food down to us here.' He laughed, setting off for the stairs.

'Unbelievable,' I said under my breath, a smile spreading across my face. Had I just then saved David from falling down the stairs?

We got to the library a few moments later. It was decked out in green and gold. A table in the front, draped in a white tablecloth, had an array of small trophies and plaques spread across it. Other tables held enormous plates of food.

'Wow!' Jimbo said, dumping his bag and racing off to the nearest table. The place was packed with people. I recognised kids, coaches and parents from the other teams in the Under 13 cricket competition. The only club that seemed thinly represented was the Scorpions. There were rumours that it was folding. Already players were looking for other clubs. Mr Smale, its owner, had supposedly disappeared up north. No one knew exactly where.

Mr Pasquali, our cricket coach, and Alistair, owner of the amazing Master Blaster virtual cricket machine, were both there. It was good to see the two of them chatting and both looking excited. Maybe Mr Pasquali was doing a deal to get the Master Blaster to school? I would definitely have a chat with him about it.

It turned out that some of the coaches, along with Dad and David, had organised for the Best and Fairest night to be held here at the MCG — in the library. They just hadn't got around to telling me. Jimbo, Scott and all the others knew.

I grabbed a seat next to Georgie when David finally got hold of the microphone to start the formal part of the evening. He told a few funny cricket stories and then passed the microphone over to Mr Pasquali, who as winning coach got the job of calling out the votes. The player with the most votes from each team automatically won their club's best and fairest. The player with the most votes won the overall Len Dalton Best Player award.

After three rounds it became pretty obvious that it was out of three players — Scott, a kid called Dean Turnbull and myself.

'You know what your problem is?' Georgie leant over and whispered in my ear, as Mr Pasquali cleared his throat to start the fourth round of votes.

'Tell me.'

'Our team was so damn good that we're all taking votes from you.' I'd had the same thought myself, but now that Georgie had spelt it out I relaxed a little. I'd had a big enough year cricket-wise — and otherwise.

Scott ended up winning.

'Geez, what's changed him?' Georgie whispered as he politely shook hands with the officials out the front. He stepped over to the microphone. From nowhere the image of Scott being taken over by a Grubber suddenly flashed into my mind, the spirit of an old cricketer somehow causing the major personality change. Shaking my head, I tried to banish the thought from my brain.

'What?' Georgie whispered.

'I'll tell you later,' I said, staring intently at Scott's face. Surely not! He began speaking.

'Um, yeah, well it's been a pretty eventful season, what with me changing clubs halfway through and everything.' He looked up and met my gaze. 'Um, I guess I really owe this to the guys at Riverwall, where I've played nearly all my cricket, and especially Toby

Jones who's shown me a few things about cricket ...' I shook my head slightly. He grinned. 'And if he and the others at Riverwall will let me come back and play then that'd be awesome.'

He stepped away from the microphone looking almost embarrassed at the long ovation he was receiving.

While Dad and David reminisced, we walked outside to the viewing area, finding a row of seats that looked out over the ground. For a while none of us spoke, each person soaking up the atmosphere of the MCG and reliving the amazing adventures of the past few months.

'I'm looking forward to staying in my own time and playing cricket,' I said finally, sighing.

'Couldn't have put it better myself.' Jimbo slapped his legs and stood up.

'Where are you going?' I asked, moving in my seat.

'Never you mind.' The others stood but Georgie suddenly squeezed my hand.

'Stay a moment longer,' she said, smiling. I shrugged, relaxing back in the seat. We sat there in silence again, gazing out over the ground. Georgie's hand was still in mine when a quiet voice started speaking from the row behind.

'Toby, my boy, you were right about that scoreboard.'

'Jim!' I cried, jumping up. Behind him was a wall of people, staring down at us and smiling, Mum, Dad

176

and Natalie in the middle of them all. They'd snuck up behind us. Slowly they moved down, but Georgie and I managed to grab the two seats on either side of him. 'The scoreboard?'

Jim nodded towards the large electronic scoreboard. 'Well, we felt it was necessary to modernise a few aspects of the Timeless Cricket Match,' he smiled. 'You'll be pleased to know that the old scoreboard is still there, but there's no need for me to be there with it.'

'And the game's going well?'

'Oh, it's chugging along at a rare old rate. There's a good crowd building and one day I'll return, as will you, Toby.'

'But not yet, Jim.'

Jim looked at me, his eyes twinkling. 'Oh no, Toby Jones. Not yet. We've much to do here first.'

'Like?' I said, suddenly fearing another frightening encounter of some sort with a spook from cricket's past.

'Well, for a start we need to get that cover drive of yours working; and then there's a leg cutter which I want you to develop —'

'Oh, is that all?'

'*Is that all?*' For the first time in ages I saw Jim laugh; really laugh. From the belly. Finally he stopped shaking. 'Well, perhaps the odd little escape to a cricket match in the past. What do you think, Toby?'

'I think that's a good idea.'

It wasn't our home ground, but it was close enough. The organisers of the Junior World Cup had scheduled cricket matches across the suburbs. International coaches and talent scouts mingled with old men walking their dogs and people strolling with pushers. It was World Cup cricket in their backyard! But Jimbo, Scott and I, the three Victorian representatives, were familiar enough with the ground. It was the Scorpions' home ground, and although we hadn't played on this particular oval, it was close enough.

We lined up opposite the New Zealand team for the national anthems.

'You reckon they'll do a haka?' Scott whispered as we moved forward to shake hands a few minutes later.

'Good luck,' I mumbled nervously, shaking hands with each of them. We had lost the toss and were fielding. I would be bowling the first over of the game.

The day was cool and overcast but there was still a huge crowd of people gathered around the ground. Cars filled the surrounding streets. Dad and Jim had arrived earlier and grabbed a great spot. I noticed that lots of other families from the Riverwall team, including Georgie, Ally and the rest of the gang, had joined them.

There was a real tension in the air and a sudden calm descended over the ground as our captain, a guy from Western Australia, made some last-minute adjustments to the field. I tossed the ball from hand to hand, looking around the oval.

'Play!' the umpire finally called, dropping his arm. Someone in the crowd started clapping and noise and excitement filled the air.

'Come on, Toby!' two deep, male voices suddenly yelled out. Despite my nerves I smiled. I knew who they were.

Two-day Ashes Test
Australia v England
Australia Ist Innings

Jimbo Temple	not out	39
Cameron Derwent	lbw Bishop	14
Callum White	b Bishop	0
Sean Robinson (c)	lbw Peterson	2
Sunil Narayanan	c Taylor b Hughes	0
Scott Craven	st Taylor b Prabakhar	18
Toby Jones	b Bishop	17
Jaimi Clayton	run out	2
Wesley Osbourne (wk)	c Hastings b Prabakhar	4
Barton Rivers	c and b Hughes	5
Greg Mackie	b Hughes	1
Extras		7
Total		**109**

FOW
35   35   41   41   62   78   85   101   104   109

England Bowling

Bishop	3 for 29
Peterson	1 for 10
Hughes	3 for 34
Prabakhar	2 for 16
Shepherd	0 for 13

England 1st Innings

Peter Lindsay	c Jones b Rivers	17
John Hastings (c)	b Rivers	30
Sebastian Crow	b Jones	0
Freddy Barnes	lbw Jones	14
Damon Shepherd	c Narayanan b Clayton	8
Sadiq Awan	c and b Jones	11
Ned Peterson	lbw Clayton	0
Bryce Taylor (wk)	c and b Jones	10
J P Prabakhar	b Jones	14
Robert Hughes	run out	3
Clayton Bishop	lbw Jones	3
Extras		12
Total		**122**

FOW
27   29   44   47   59   59   78   91   117   122

Australia Bowling

Jones	6 for 30
Rivers	2 for 34
Craven	0 for 9
Mackie	0 for 14
Clayton	2 for 21

Australia 2nd Innings

Jimbo Temple	c Taylor b Bishop	91
Cameron Derwent	run out	41
Scott Craven	c Shepherd b Peterson	24
Callum White	b Prabakhar	7
Sean Robinson (c)	lbw Prabakhar	8
Sunil Narayanan	c Bishop b Prabakhar	1
Toby Jones	c Taylor b Bishop	5
Jaimi Clayton	c Crow b Prabakhar	2
Wesley Osbourne (wk)	not out	4
Barton Rivers	dnb	

Greg Mackie	dnb	
Extras		5
Total		**8 / 188**

FOW

123   140   153   155   161   171   185   188

England Bowling

Bishop	2 for 47
Peterson	1 for 31
Hughes	0 for 29
Prabakhar	4 for 76

England 2nd Innings

Peter Lindsay	lbw Jones	22
John Hastings (c)	b Jones	25
Sebastian Crow	c Clayton b Craven	7
Freddy Barnes	b Rivers	10
Damon Shepherd	c McCabe b Jones	7
Sadiq Awan	c Rivers b Jones	1
Ned Peterson	hit the ball twice	0
Bryce Taylor (wk)	b Jones	0
J P Prabakhar	b Craven	4
Robert Hughes	c and b Craven	4
Clayton Bishop	lbw Craven	3
Extras		8
Total		**91**

FOW

36   39   48   51   60   60   60   77   86   91

Australia Bowling

Jones	5 for 31
Craven	4 for 34
Clayton	0 for 12
Rivers	0 for 6

Underarm bowling

In the early days of cricket, all bowling was underarm. There was fast bowling, slow bowling, spin bowling and lobs, where the bowler tried to land the ball on top of the stumps, but it was all underarm bowling. Female cricketers of the nineteenth century wore wide skirts and couldn't bowl underarm because of the dress. So instead, they bowled with a roundarm style.

People watching quickly realised what a powerful technique this was. The ball could be delivered more quickly and the pitch could be used to extract bounce and turn. It was banned for a while but people realised the game was more exciting with this style of bowling. Roundarm bowling soon turned into overarm bowling. This all happened about 150 years ago — well before the first *Wisden* was published!

The most famous underarm delivery was bowled by Trevor Chappell in a one-day game for Australia against New Zealand in 1981. New Zealand needed six runs off the last ball to tie the game, so the Australian captain, Greg Chappell, told his younger brother to bowl an underarm delivery — a grubber that rolled along the pitch and would be impossible to hit in the air. The New Zealand batter, Brian McKechnie, blocked it, then threw his bat away in disgust. After this, underarm bowling was banned from all grades of cricket.

Nightwatchmen

A nightwatchman is a lower order batter who comes in to protect a higher order batter, usually because a wicket has fallen near the end of the day's play. Rather than risk losing another wicket in the final few overs, the captain sometimes decides to send in one of his bowlers. His job is just to survive until stumps. He will hopefully be not out and remain in overnight — which is where the term comes from.

Nightwatchmen are not really meant to make big scores — often they are dismissed early the next day. But if they survive the evening, they have done their job.

There have been some famous nightwatchmen scores. The highest-ever score by a nightwatchman was made by Jason Gillespie for Australia against Bangladesh at Chittagong in 2006. He made a massive 201 not out.

Here are the best nightwatchmen scores:

Player	Team	Score	Versus	Ground	Date
Jason Gillespie	Australia	201 not out	Bangladesh	Chittagong Divisional Stadium, Chittagong, Bangladesh	2006
Tony Mann	Australia	108	India	WACA Ground, Perth, Western Australia	1977
Nasim-ul-Ghani	Pakistan	101	England	Lord's, London, England	1962

Alex Tudor made 99 not out for England against New Zealand in 1999 at Edgbaston.

THE 10 WAYS OF BEING DISMISSED

1. Bowled
2. Caught
3. Hit wicket
4. Stumped
5. LBW (leg before wicket)
6. Run out
7. Handled the ball
8. Hit the ball twice
9. Obstructing the field
10. Timed out

The bowler gets the credit for the wicket for methods 1–5.

A batter can retire – and is considered not out. He might be injured and unable to complete his innings. If he gets better, he can come back in at the fall of a wicket.

There is a very mysterious eleventh way to be given out. It's if you retire by agreement with the opposition captain, perhaps to give another batter on your team a hit. If the retired batter doesn't go back in, the scorecard would say 'retired – out'.

A player in Pakistan, playing in the Quaid-e-Azam Trophy for Karachi against Pakistan Combined Services in the 1958–59 competition, was hit on the chest by a delivery. He died on the way to hospital. There's a rumour that the scorecard looked like this:

> 1st innings: Abdul Aziz, retired hurt, 0
> 2nd innings: Abdul Aziz, did not bat, dead, 0

This could be a twelfth way of recording a dismissal, but the rumour is untrue. The official scorecard showed the player as 'absent'.

10 QUESTIONS FOR BRETT LEE

- *What do you do to prepare yourself when you are next in to bat?*
  I get a little nervous but only enough to make sure my mind is sharp. I sit and watch what the bowlers are doing out in the middle and work out how I plan to play them.

- *How do you control your nerves when you are about to bowl?*
  I get more nervous when I am about to bat! I take a few deep breaths at the end of my mark and focus on where I want the ball to pitch. I get my thoughts clear as to what delivery I want to bowl and then I concentrate on my approach and release.

- *How can I make my run-up smoother? I'm always worried I'm going to bowl no balls.*
  Measuring your run is important. We tend to practise our run-ups and with a tape measure or piece of string record the distance, although you need to take into account the 'sponginess' of the grass, as well as how flat the ground is. These things impact on the length of your running stride. Keeping your head still will impact on the smoothness of your run-up.

- *Have you ever been a nightwatchman and how did you go?*
  I have been nightwatchman on a couple of occasions. I did quite well a few times, managing to bat through the session and then hanging around the next morning. Although, I did remember getting a golden duck once, which didn't really help the team or my average!

- *What do you do to stay focused if you are out injured?*
  Depending on the injury, I train harder. If I can't run, I swim, or I will find other ways to stay fit. By doing this I reduce my recovery time once I'm given the okay to play.

- *How can I work on my batting if I'm a fast bowler?*
  My initial focus was to just not get out. I learnt a lot from watching Jason Gillespie's approach. He just stayed in and then the runs started to come either for him or his partner. The longer you are in, the more confidence you get. In short, don't try and play all the shots – minimise the risk of getting out.

- *Do you talk much to the opposition on the field and what do you say?*
  I am not a 'talker'. I will chat occasionally but only on a social level. There are times when I need to intimidate, but that is normally done through not saying anything.

- *Does having the best gear make you a better player?*
  No – Don Bradman had a second-hand bat when he scored his first triple century and he was definitely the best player ever! Good equipment can definitely help, but by no means does 'old gear' mean you are a worse player.

- *Who's the toughest batsman you've ever had to bowl to and why?*
  Generally speaking it is Brian Lara and Sachin Tendulkar, but I'll never forget the occasion I was bowling to Chris Cairns in a Test match. He was on song! It didn't matter where anyone bowled it, he was smashing them.

- *Are you going to be a musician when you leave cricket?*
  I love my music and I hope one day to be able to spend more time playing and singing. You never know!

Glossary

bails Two small pieces of wood that sit on top of the stumps. At least one has to fall off the stumps for a bowled or run-out decision to be made.

centre-wicket practice Team practice played out on a cricket field, as opposed to in the nets. Sometimes two or more bowlers are used, one after the other, to speed up the practice. If the batter goes out, he or she usually stays on for more batting practice.

covers A fielding position on the side of the wicket that the batter is facing, halfway between the bowler and the wicket keeper.

crease There are quite a few creases in cricket. They are lines drawn near the stumps that help the batters and bowlers know where they are in relation to the stumps.

fine leg A fielding position down near the boundary line behind the wicket keeper. Often a fast bowler fields in this position.

gully A close-in fielding position along from the slips — the fielders next to the wicket keeper.

lbw Stands for 'leg before wicket'. This is a way for a batter to be dismissed. If the bowler hits the pads of the batter with the ball, and he or she thinks that the ball would have gone on and hit the stumps, then the bowler can appeal for lbw. If the umpire is sure that the batter didn't hit the ball with the bat, then the batter may be given out.

leg-stump There are three stumps. This is the stump that is nearest the legs of the batter.

maiden If a bowler bowls an over and no runs are scored from it, then it is called a maiden.

mid-off A fielding position next to the bowler. It is on the off or bat side of the pitch as the batter looks down the wicket.

mid-on A fielding position next to the bowler. It is on the on or leg side of the pitch as the batter looks down the wicket.

no ball If a bowler puts his or her foot entirely over the return crease (the marked line) then it is a no ball and the batter can't be given out — unless it is a run-out.

off-stump The stump that is on the batting side of the batter.

third man A fielding position down behind the wicket keeper but on the other side of the fine leg fielder. The third man fielder is behind the slips fielders.

yorker The name for a delivery, usually bowled by a medium or fast bowler, that is pitched right up near the batter's feet. It is full pitched and fast.

Acknowledgments

Thanks to Robert McVicker Burmeister for his involvement with the cover. To John Wisden & Co. Ltd for their kind assistance, and for the wealth of information contained in the *Wisden Cricketers' Almanack*s. To Peter Young at Cricket Australia for his support and suggestions. Thanks to the staff at the Insite Organisation for their tremendous support for the Toby series. To the wonderful and knowledgeable David Studham at the MCC Library, now even further involved in the plot and whose character is growing in stature; if Toby 6 eventuates, David will author it! To the superb staff at HarperCollins whose patience and tireless enthusiasm have made the five-year Toby Jones journey so enjoyable and rewarding. Special thanks in particular to Lisa Berryman, Liz Kemp and Patrick Mangan — a friendlier and more professional team would be very hard to find.

Michael Panckridge has worked as a teacher just over twenty years and currently teaches part-time at Geelong College. He has been a lifelong fan of all sports, especially cricket. Michael has both played and coached cricket but is quite sure he has never clocked a speed at even half the pace that Brett Lee bowls at.

**Visit Michael's website at
www.michaelpanckridge.com.au**

BRETT LEE grew up in Wollongong, New South Wales, and is the younger brother of former international cricketing all-rounder Shane Lee. Brett made his first-class cricketing debut in 1995 and his Australian debut against India in 1999/2000. He is one of the country's fastest ever bowlers, regularly clocking speeds of over 150 kilometres per hour.

Toby Jones and the
Magic Cricket Almanack

MICHAEL PANCKRIDGE

WITH BRETT LEE

Toby Jones and his friends are obsessed with cricket. They all play in the Under-13 school team and hang out in their own online cricket chatroom after school. Luckily, they also have a sports-mad teacher who lets them do projects on cricket.

While on a school excursion Toby visits the Melbourne Cricket Club Library, where he meets fellow cricket buff Jim Oldfield and stumbles upon the secret of the Magic Cricket Almanack. This secret, which Jim shares, is so extraordinary it could change Toby's life forever.

Life for Toby and his friends becomes a balancing act — following their passion of playing cricket while keeping Toby's new-found secret. But are they ready for the dangers this secret holds?

Toby Jones and the Magic Cricket Almanack is the first book in an exciting new series that combines cricket with fantasy. Featuring cricket commentary co-written with Australian fast bowler Brett Lee, this is a book guaranteed to leave you wanting more.

Toby Jones and the Secret of the Missing Scorecard

MICHAEL PANCKRIDGE

WITH BRETT LEE

Toby Jones lives and breathes cricket. He plays in a local cricket competition, follows the professional players and knows all the stats. But Toby has a secret — he can travel back through time to watch famous cricket matches and players. And he can take his friends with him. But it's not all good news ...

There are dangers. Toby has seen the strange, hooded figure lurking in the background. What, or who, is this creepy character after? And how desperate is he to get what he wants?

If you love fantasy or sport, you'll love reading the Toby Jones books.

'Kids, cricket, fun — always the perfect combination.' BRETT LEE

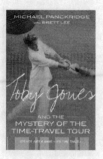

Toby Jones and the
Mystery of the Time-Travel Tour

MICHAEL PANCKRIDGE

WITH BRETT LEE

Toby Jones is not your average cricket fan — he can travel
through time, back to the great matches of the past. When his
friend and fellow time traveller Jim Oldfield is left behind —
last seen watching Bradman play at Leeds in 1930 — Toby
knows he's the only one who can find Jim.

Meanwhile, Phillip Smale, ruthless team manager of the rival
Scorpions, is working on a secretive scheme to lure rich cricket-
lovers to his Timeless Travel Tours ... but there is no guarantee
of a return ticket.

Can Toby save Jim and also thwart Smale's perilous plan?
Or will the dangers of time travelling lead to disaster?

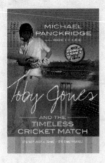

Toby Jones and the
Timeless Cricket Match

MICHAEL PANCKRIDGE

WITH BRETT LEE

It isn't Toby Jones' passion for cricket that makes him unusual —
it's his ability to travel through time, back to the great matches of
the past.

Just when Toby thinks his time-travel adventures are over, he
has to make another dangerous journey. He must travel to The
Oval — the famous English cricket ground — to save his friend
Ally, who has been ill since she broke the laws of time travel on
her last trip with him.

Toby will have to face the embittered Cricket Lord, Hugo
Malchev, and the ruthless Phillip Smale, who has his own
agenda as far as time travel is concerned, and doesn't want
anyone getting in the way.

And if that isn't enough, Toby is training at the cricket camp
at the Melbourne Cricket Ground, hoping to be selected for
Australia against England in the junior Ashes. If he doesn't get
stuck in the past during his travels. Or worse . . .